Gargoyle's Spring

Gracie Cooper

ISBN: 9798875576096

This book is a work of fiction. Names, characters, places and incidents are products of the author's imagination or are used fictitiously and are not to be construed as real. Any resemblance to actual events, locales, organizations, or people, living or dead, is entirely coincidental.

Cover Design By: Isabelle Olmo

www.graciecooper.com

Dedicated to Joanna and Philip
With all my love

Chapter One
Frick Frack Toad's Tongue

"No, no, no, no, no, no," Ibis Heliodoro groaned over and over, fanning her hands through the hazy, green smoke. Desperately, she searched for a resolution to the error she made with her spell. "Frick, frack, toad's tongue," she muttered, gagging at the wretched smell of aged garlic and some unworldly stench exuding from the paisley flowers. All she wanted to do was change the dying poinsettias into gardenias.

Defeated, she looked at the gawking eyes of her familiar Sooty, the astute owl, Kit, the protective fox, and Chaos, the mischievous speckled cat.

Among them, far in the back on the upper level, frozen in stone, with a disapproving stare, was Oliver. He was the resident gargoyle of the library. An elusive library hidden from the mundane world. Only witches had permission to enter. Well, only witches who could perform magic were allowed to enter the sacred library.

What witch cannot do magic, some may ask?

Ibis Heliodoro.

That witch.

It didn't matter if she carried the prestigious last name, Heliodoro. A prominent name passed down by generations of strong Light

Witches. Somehow, the magic bypassed her and went astray somewhere else.

Although still considered a witch, Ibis was not a good one. Clarification, Ibis Heliodoro was a *good witch*. She just was not good at magic. Every spell, hex, incantation, whatever magical invocation she performed always went wrong.

Always.

So much so, the Countess herself, none other than her *Tia,* cast Ibis out of the esteemed Coven and banished her into the confinements of the library, bringing shame to the Heliodoro name.

Ibis was demoted to keeper of the pivotal documents, records, books and time lines. Keeper of sealed secrets only a seasoned prominent witch of The Order could open. Keeper of the Onyx Key, which opened the lock to the Golden Keys.

Which meant Ibis was a glorified librarian. One who was about to set the whole frick frack sacred library on fire because she was feeling the season change to spring and wanted to decorate the old, crusty room with gardenias and fairy lights. Goddess, she loved gardenias and fairy lights.

Whoever wrote these ingredients had poor penmanship.

The sounds of wings flapping around her head distracted her. From above, Sooty dropped a bottle from her enormous claws. Ibis fumbled with the bottle, securing it with both hands. She blew a frustrated breath, flinging her long auburn wave of hair from her face. In small print, it read cleansing oil. Ibis arched her brow at Sooty, who swiveled her neck around, as if saying, "What are you waiting for?" More green smoke and stench rose from the paisley flowers.

Ibis tucked her nose in the collar of her blouse's neckline. Coughing and gagging, she read the instructions. Then again. Then once more. Three drops only, and the stench would be eliminated.

"Here goes nothing," she muttered under her breath. "One," she issued the first tear drop. "Two," the second one followed, causing a fizzle. Smiling for the first time since the disaster. "Three," she chirped.

The green smoke stopped. The sudden smells of coconut oil and lemon infused the air. Sighing with relief, she sealed the cleansing oil and held it up in the air for the Sooty to retrieve it. Sooty snatched the bottle from Ibis's hand, held it in its claws, and flew it to the top shelves where all the bottles were kept alongside its perch.

She twirled with excitement. "I did it."

"Hooot," mocked Sooty.

Fine. "We did it."

Ibis cleaned the contaminated area, covering the scent with lavender, or rather spraying down the areas with lavender scented cleaner. Safe for her to use and not damage or destroy any important books within the library. She wiped the table tops as Kit moved around the large spiral stairwell, racing to the third floor and tapping on the radio Ibis kept tucked away. Music blared out of the speakers. Her fluffy tail swished back and forth to Taylor Swifts 'Anti-Hero'. A song picked out for her.

"Very funny," Ibis mumbled, side-eying Kit. The little devious animals were her sole companions behind the large, quiet walls. Them and the handsome stone guardian himself.

Walls filled the room from floor to ceiling with books ranging from healing and health spells to protections and wards. The sacred library divided into different sections. A pair of large oak doors with the witches' mark carved within the wood greeted those allowed inside. Once inside, a massive floating arch with crystal blue water circling the stones and falling into an unknown abyss of mist on the floor greeted visitors. Ghostly luminescence filtered from the mist, illuminating the surrounding floor, lighting a path with its mystique blue light towards to the center, where the library divided into five pivotal hallways.

Ibis always wondered where the water flowed. What world did it belong to? Could they go there? According to the legends, the arch was a doorway to another dimension. Another world.

Beyond the arch there were the first two hallways, one on the right and one on the left. Each had a black wrought iron spiral staircase leading to the above floors. Further in, another set of hallways split. The last hallway was across from the arch, and in the middle sat Ibis. A simple writer's desk made of oak, with twisted and turned legs. Carved vines decorated the wood. A clear glass protected the etched wood where Ibis cataloged the books.

Manually.

Yes, manually. Nothing was operated with modern technology in the library. As advanced as the witches were with magic, technology was not something they were up to speed with. In fact, it was frowned upon to even own a phone. Especially in the library. Although Ibis kept a tablet hidden away in her quarters. She loved watching the mundane shows. Oh, how comical she found their love for the supernatural world.

If they only knew. She sighed, her eyes drifting to the arch.

She loved looking at the arch. She would stare at it for hours. After all, it was right in front of her. Then there were times she swiveled her chair and stared at the endless hallway of darkness where

8

a pair of sealed doors waited to be unlocked by the Golden Keys. Of course, staring at a pair of sealed doors was not what she found intriguing. Her trusted, handsome stone friend, Oliver, sat perched on the ledge above the door. His wings expanded, encasing the entire entry. Claws loomed over the ledge, holding him upright. Sharp features etched the stone, detailing his nose and pointed ears. Someone would say he was handsome. That someone would be her. Well, not mostly. It would all be her. But why wouldn't he be? Regardless of how old the aged stonework was, Oliver nicely preserved himself. His features were almost human, like in other worldly way. An uncanny stare remained in his eyes as if he watched the library. Armor covered parts of his torso and lower frame. The ridges on his arms reflected strength. Even perched, he towered over Ibis. Many times, Ibis climbed up and sat next to him or even on his stoned lap and chatted about her day or just watched her tablet. She felt so small next to him.

Small.

Something she had never felt. According to the mundane standard, she would be a plus size witch. Whatever the hex that meant. She never could understand the fixation on weight. She was who she was, and she loved it. Witches came in every shape, color, and size. Ibis rocked her wavy auburn hair, curvy figure and dark brown eyes. It didn't matter if her nose was slightly crooked because of a mishap with an exploding spell.

The important thing was magic.

Unfortunately for her, magic was just not in her blood. Technically, it was, but it was quirky, hexed and bat shit crazy.

What man wanted a jinxed witch?

Better she stick with her familiars, books and her friend Oliver. He didn't care if she was a complete screw up. He never judged. He never questioned her. He was perfect for her. Then again, he never spoke either.

She stared at Oliver longingly. "I guess that would be the case if they made you from stone."

She was in trouble. Big, big trouble. The kind of trouble where the order was called together to discuss misdeeds, misconduct and misjudgment. The three M's or the MMM or better yet the *mmm* meeting. Ibis hated these meetings. Mandatory attendance was required by all residents.

All residents.

This meant all residents, regardless of what level of practiced magic was required to attend. Which included Ibis.

She was a witch.

A resident.

No doubt she committed a misdeed misconduct and definitely misjudged her ability for magic.

Frick, frack, toad's tongues.

"What's got you all frazzled?" whispered her dear friend Elizabeth. During her freakout moment, Elizabeth secured a spot next to her. Long platinum blonde hair with bright pink highlights hung over her shoulders in a thick braid. Her dark, gentle eyes lit up with excitement.

Why did Elizabeth enjoy these wretched meetings she would never understand?

"Who's frazzled?" a hoarse whisper came from her other side. Wherever Elizabeth was, her twin brother Andrew would be nearby. As in identical twin brother, except for pink tips in his hair. Their magic was linked as twins. Together, their magic was powerful, something many witches envied.

"I'm not frazzled."

He dropped his eyes down, tilting his head, arching his dark brow and smirking, standing almost a foot taller than her. "You're a horrible liar."

"I'm not lying," Ibis whisper-yelled.

"She's lying," they both said.

"Shhhh," Selma scolded.

Ibis mouthed an apology to Selma while Elizabeth rolled her eyes, and Andrew made a childish face.

Selma Abbott was a witch of the order. A witch to be respected and revered. A witch Ibis looked up to and hoped to be one day. Not to mention, a witch who not only was powerful, but was gorgeous with her dark curls and strands of gray teasing her hair. She was tall and slim, with full lips and moss like eyes. Eyes that were all-knowing, all-seeing and all-dangerous. It was no wonder she was mated to The Veil Force commander, Azrael. A reaper.

"Looks like someone can't take a joke," muttered Andrew, still turning and skewing his face.

"Andrew stop," warned Ibis.

"What?" he said, rolling his eyes back and letting his tongue hang out to the side.

11

"Andrew," Elizabeth mumbled.

A sudden chill crept up Ibis's arm. Her warm breath froze in the air, as did Elizabeth's. They looked at each other wide-eyed.

"Andrew," they both said louder as a dark, ghostly figure crawled around the wall behind them, inching its way.

Red eyes glowed.

Claws scraped the wall.

Elizabeth leaned closer to Ibis. Both reaching for Andrew before the shadow did.

Red eyes turned to them, and it snarled.

They jumped, leaping into Andrew's back.

"What in the..." Andrew turned his head and frowned down at Ibis and Elizabeth. Ibis reached up on her pointed toes and turned his head forward to face the red-eyed ghost.

"Ibis, what are you do...oh, hey Azrael," he said, his voice turning a pitch higher than normal.

The red-eyed ghost transformed into a six-foot two man. His eyes glowed in his skeleton face. Bony hands raised behind his head, lifting the hood from his cloak and covering his skull face. Within seconds, the magic of the cloak gave life to his skeleton figure.

"Stop flirting with my mate," Azrael hissed.

"I wasn't flirting. I was just..."

Azrael conjured his scythe, raising it high on the ground and slamming the bottom to the ground. A circle formed around Andrew's feet.

"Yup. You got it. No more flirty, funny faces at your, uh, your mate. Message received," Andrew stuttered.

Ibis peeked over Andrew's shoulder while Elizabeth did the same on the other.

"We can take him," Elizabeth said in a hush voice.

Ibis rolled her eyes, admiring the way Azrael slid a possessive arm around Selma's small waist and pulled her closer. The way Selma's face turned soft, staring into his eyes. The way they leaned into each other and shared a secret conversation only mates could hear with one and another. The way Selma caressed the heart shape necklace she wore close to her chest.

"You two don't stand a chance against either of them," Ibis mumbled.

Andrew crossed his arms and grumbled, "Whatever."

They walked a little closer into the crowd. Andrew and Elizabeth both avoided Selma and Azrael, leaving Ibis to stand next to them. She glanced shyly over at them and earned a small smile from Selma and a wink from Azrael.

Ibis turned to her two close friends with a brilliant smile as if saying, see they're not so bad, only to look back and see them both scowling at Elizabeth and Andrew.

Jupiter's balls.

Who needs mundane television shows when there was drama live at The Veil?

Chapter Two

Not Invited

C andlelight flickered, brightening the room. A hush fell around them. One by one, the Order approached the front. Azrael stayed behind, standing close to Ibis. He glanced down at her, eyes now a pink hue, sparkling with mischief, and rolled them. She coughed a laugh and lowered her head, not wanting to be caught. She glanced up and Selma smirked. Ibis did like Selma and Azrael. They never made her feel like an outcast. Neither did Elizabeth nor Andrew. They were the few who she could really call friends.

"We call this meeting to order."

Two booming pounds echoed as The Veil Force slammed the bottom of their weapons to the floor.

Ibis glanced at her feet. No circles formed around her after Azrael slammed his scythe this time.

Interesting.

"As all are aware, spring is upon us," said the Countess. "The Ostara Ball was to be held at Briar's Solarium. There was an unfortunate incident and The Briars can no longer host the Ball."

Murmurs of disappointment filtered through the room. Everyone who attended The Ostara Ball loved going to Briar's Solarium. It was a beautiful, secluded location. Not that Ibis ever attended. She had only seen the visions shared by Elizabeth and Andrew.

Oh, but how she would have loved to have gone this year.

The Countess raised her hands, silencing the room. A giant smile broke her face. "The Veil will host The Ostara Ball this year."

Loud gasps and excitement buzzed around the room. Elizabeth bounced on her heels. Andrew looked ready to puke.

"The Order will delegate roles to members of our coven. We have little time to prepare. Guests will arrive within a night's time. Our house must be in order by then."

Everyone agreed, and The Veil Force pounded their weapons on the ground, acknowledging the order.

"Dismissed," she said with a wave of her hand.

"Can you believe it?" squealed Elizabeth. "We have to go shopping." Ibis nodded.

"This sucks Jupiter's balls," grumbled Andrew.

"Ew," Elizabeth said with a grotesque sneer.

Ibis giggled, but remained quiet. Her eyes stared at the Countess. Her *Tia*.

Will she acknowledge her?

Will she even look at her?

Just a look, *Tia*.

Just one.

"Hello? Are you listening to me?"

Ibis blinked and turned to Elizabeth. "Sorry, I didn't hear you."

Elizabeth turned and sighed, catching on to what Ibis was staring at. "She still hasn't talked to you?"

"No."

"Who's not talking to you?" asked Andrew.

"She won't even look at me," Ibis said.

"I'm so sorry," soft petite arms wrapped around her.

"Who are we gossiping about?" whisper-yelled Andrew. "It's not Selma right? Because I almost got ghosted by that red-eye fucker."

"I don't stay in our quarters anymore. I sleep in the library."

Both hands came up to Elizabeth's mouth. Andrew's hands turned into fists. "Alright now, I don't know what is going on, but you will not be living in the library. You can stay with us," he said, grinding his teeth.

"He's right. Come stay with us. We can make it work."

Ibis shook her head. She loved them. She did, but the rules were simple. There was a reason for pairing everyone into living quarters together. It was one thing to stay for a night or two, but to live there long term required approval from The Order. Everything had a reason at The Veil and no one questioned it.

Since she was the librarian, there was no reason she couldn't live in the only place she ever felt needed and wanted in. Among the dust, cobwebs and ancient scriptures, she found an empty, shady loft which was even dustier, with more cobwebs and shadier bathroom. At least the plumbing worked. With the help of her familiars, she cleaned up the area and converted the decrepit space into a cozy room full of books, warmth and comfort.

"It's alright. I really like it there. I even have a little fireplace."

Elizabeth stared at her in horror.

"Will it blow up if you light it?" Andrew asked.

Ibis shoved him. "No. It works just fine."

"But it's lonely in there."

Ibis smiled sadly at Elizabeth. She wasn't lying. "I'm not that lonely. Witches come in all the time for books. Plus, I have Sooty, Chaos and Kit. Oh, and Oliver. He's there."

"Who?"

"The gargoyle," Ibis and Elizabeth said.

"Now I'm worried about you," he grumbled.

"Ignore him. He's cranky. He doesn't want the ball to be here because of a certain Briar Witch he screwed around with last season." Elizabeth snickered.

"She has nothing to do with it."

"Sure brother. Keep telling yourself that." Elizabeth snickered. "She almost set his crotch on fire for sneaking out of her quarters without saying goodbye," she whispered.

"Andrew!" Ibis scolded

"What? I had to leave, and I didn't want to wake her. I left a note."

"That is so wrong," Ibis said, shaking her head, walking out of the hallway, forgetting about her aunt.

"Don't be disappointed in me," he said grumblingly to Ibis.

She giggled. Oh Andrew.

"Shameful," she said, making him blush.

"So shameful," Elizabeth parroted.

"Look who's talking, Ms. I'm In Love With A Fictional Character," Andrew teased in a high-pitched voice mocking Elizabeth.

Ibis's jaw dropped.

"You are such a snitch!" Elizabeth cried.

"Ha. Says the twin who ratted me out."

"Come on Ibis. Let's go before I forget I need his dumbass for magic."

Ibis followed Elizabeth. Well, not like she didn't have a choice since Elizabeth dragged her out of the room down the hall to the exit.

"Wait. Where are you going?" Andrew grumbled, catching up to them.

"Shopping. With my best friend," Elizabeth snapped.

"She's my best friend, too. Plus, I need to go shopping."

"Dress shopping?"

"I can give you all my honest opinions on your dresses," he said with a wicked smile.

"Ha! Like I need them," Elizabeth snapped back.

Ibis threw her hands in the air. These two, when they got along, it was great, but when they argued over things, even the pettiest of things, it was soul sucking, draining.

Frick frack toad's tongue.

"Enough!" Ibis demanded, silencing them both. "Either both of you go or I won't go at all."

They stared at each other forever. Perhaps a minute, but to Ibis it felt forever. Andrew stuck his hand out in a truce. Elizabeth squinted her eyes and then rolled them, bringing her hand out to shake it only for Andrew to pull it back and running it through his hair like an adolescent. "Too slow punk."

Elizabeth growled and pushed Andrew with both her hands. "You are such a big, hairy dick sometimes, you know that."

Andrew chuckled and grabbed her hands, pulling her into his arms and squeezing his sister tight. "Yeah, but you love me. Big, hairy dick and all."

"Ew, you are so gross," Elizabeth muttered in his chest, trying to break free from his embrace.

He switched her over in one arm and with his now free arm, hooked Ibis around her neck and brought her into his bear hug. "Come on. Let's go dress shopping for my two dates," he said, all too happily.

Excitement bloomed in Ibis's belly. Dress shopping for The Ostara Ball. Who would have thought? This would be her first Ostara Ball. Her first ball. The last dance was the Winter Solstice. She stood on the library's balcony and watched as everyone made their way out of the back gates into The Veil's Stone Garden, where Azrael's men kept watch over the stone pillars. Only those with invitation could pass the stone pillars into the garden. She was not one of them. Like a creeper in the night, she snuck out to the balcony and climbed up, sitting on the roof's ledge. Watching and listening to the laugher and music of the gala, while eating a pint of ice cream.

Maybe she should stock up on her ice cream while she was out and get those cookies Sooty liked. Her little owl had a sweet tooth.

"Ibis?"

She froze. Her eyes locked with four shocked ones staring back at her. She slowly turned around and came face to face with the Countess.

Her *Tia*.

Isa Heliodoro.

"Hi *Tia*," she whispered, unsure how to address her.

She pursed her lips and folded her hands. "*¿A dónde vas?*"

Right to the point. "I was going to go with Elizabeth and Andrew to town."

Elizabeth squeezed her hand. "We are going dress shopping, Countess Isa. We will return before sunset."

Andrew stepped forward, standing next to Ibis. Never touching her, but remaining close.

"Dress shopping? Whatever for?"

Ibis's smile faltered. She swallowed the knot forming in the back of her throat. Her breath caught. Suddenly, the room seemed small and hard to breathe. All eyes turned to stare, whispering among themselves.

Selma and Azrael trudged forward. The look in their eyes stabbed her heart.

Pity.

She was far too aware of that look. In their hands, they each held an envelope. They were invitations.

Selma placed an invitation in Elizabeth's hand and another in Andrew's. Her moss-like eyes met Ibis filled with sadness and something else Ibis could not read. Maybe it was more than pity. Maybe Selma felt embarrassed for her. Maybe it was anger. At the moment, Ibis couldn't figure out the emotion.

Ibis nodded slightly, understanding.

"Ibis will not be needing a dress. She will not be attending The Ostara Ball," announced the Countess for all to hear.

Ibis's cheeks burned with humiliation. Being denied discreetly was one thing, but publicly rejected by your own family was another.

The questioning whispers were much louder than expected. Or maybe that was exactly what they wanted. *Why is she being denied? Is she an outcast?*

The answer was simple. Not only did Ibis Heliodoro have broken magic, but she also denied her pairing with an acceptable mate. A mate who would grant Ibis powers and accept her back into the coven. A mate, chosen by her Tia Isa.

Frick frack.

As if she would ever consider mating with Elton Salas.

Chapter Three
The Mean Witch

C urled up in her favorite chair, she scooped another spoonful of ice cream and flipped the page of her current romance novel. After the humiliation of earlier events, Ibis escaped the scrutinizing stares and sideway smiles from the resident mean girls. She disregarded Elizabeth and Andrew's calls to come with them, despite what her *Tia* had said. She ignored Selma and Azrael's pity looks. She ignored Elton's smirk as she walked past him. But most of all, she ignored her *Tia's* disapproving glare.

She lost herself in her book, dreaming of sailing away with the hero as they searched for ancient relics in the high seas, evading the dangers of mother nature and pirates. Sometimes sailing through a storm sounded better than being at The Veil.

The creaky library door opened. With a heavy heart, Ibis swallowed the last bit of her spoonful and returned her ice cream back to its place. She located her shoes and folded the blanket, only for Kit to whine. She chuckled and unfolded the blanket again and covered up the spoiled little fox. Chaos purred from the banister. Her fluffy tail swished back and forth. Yellow eyes blinked lazily. Poor Sooty snored away on her perch.

"I can't believe she really thought she was going to the ball. She can't even do magic."

Ugh.

Of all Witches to come into the library now, it had to be Mona Gil. The Gil's were part of the Light Witches. Like the Heliodoro, they came from a long line of witches. And of course, Mona believed she was the ultimate Light Witch.

Why?

Because, like Ibis, Mona was born from a powerful match. A match approved by the Light Goddess herself. And just like Ibis, Mona was next in line to join the Order. However, unlike Ibis, Mona's magic was strong and accurate.

Although Ibis was strong in other areas, her magic was not. It was a hot train wreck on wheels, cruising down tracks made of melted candle wax.

"To think, they paired her with Elton."

Yes. *Tia* ensured Ibis was paired with Elton.

Elton Salas was the poster boy for handsome. If witches had their own magazine, Elton Salas would be on the cover with his perfectly cut brown hair, perfectly plucked eyebrows and perfectly flawless fair skin. He was the epitome of perfection. The complete opposite of what she was. But that was not the reason Ibis turned him down. For all his good looks, pristine wardrobe, perfectly manicured hands and styled hair, Elton Salas was the biggest jerk face of all jerk faces. Just hearing his voice made her skin crawl. She'd rather be paired to a troll than be paired to him.

"Mona, it's not nice to talk about your cousin that way."

"Please. We are barely related."

Ibis wrinkled her nose. Regla was close friends with Mona. They were paired together. Regardless, Regla was never mean to Ibis.

Indifferent maybe.

But never mean.

"Why are we here, anyway?" Regla asked, hands on her hips as she glanced around the room.

"I heard Elton say he was coming by the library," Mona said with a shrug, tossing back her long, straight chestnut hair.

"You don't think he's coming to ask her to the ball?"

Mona laughed loudly. "Really Regla? *Tia* Isa said she's not allowed. Besides, Ibis is not a witch. She's a freaking disgrace. I don't know why *Tia* Isa even allows her to remain here. Someone should cast her out."

Ibis stopped halfway down the stairs, hiding behind Oliver's massive wings. She leaned her head against him and stifled a cry.

An outcast? Is that what everyone thought of her?

"That's not nice, Mona. No one deserves that."

Mona rolled her eyes and looked around. Her eyes peering directly at the gargoyle. "Then maybe someone should turn her to stone and take her out of her misery."

The last shot from her words caused Ibis to gasp. Tears flowed freely down her face. Sooty shot from her perch, screeching down the opening towards Mona with her talons exposed.

Mona screamed, batting her arms around wildly as Sooty continue to claw at her. Regla tried to pull Sooty off, only to be scratched at the legs by Chaos. "You vicious cat," she snapped back. Both Mona and Regla joined hands. Eyes glowing, the surrounding air fizzled and electrified. Energy surged in the palms of each of their hands as they raised them up to fire at Sooty and Chaos.

"No!" Ibis cried out. "Don't hurt them." She raced down the stairs. Kit following behind her. Kit jumped in front of Chaos, teeth exposed and chattering away with her noises. Fussing at them for what they were doing.

Mona looked at Ibis and smiled wickedly. She aimed her hand at Sooty and shot one electric bolt, missing as Sooty dodged to the right. Hooting and screeching at her. The bolt hit Oliver's wing, clipping the top, releasing a crumble of stones to the ground.

"Mona, please stop. You'll hurt them," Ibis pleaded.

Ignoring her, Mona took aim as Regla held back, her eyes losing its flare, filling with regret. She turned to calm Mona.

"Mona, stop," Regla demanded. It only enraged Mona more.

Another bolt shot out of Mona and hit nothing. It vanished. Mona growled loudly and released Regla's hand. The surge of energy evaporated. Behind them, Selma stood with her hands up, green eyes glowing as her shields protected the library. Azrael charged in, along with his second in command, Tyzion.

"What is the meaning of this?" demanded Azrael, his cloak shaded his face, giving him the power to hide his Reaper features. His eyes glowed red.

Heaving heavily, Mona pointed at Sooty, who perched herself back on the banister. She swirled her neck around and flapped her wings angrily while Chaos arched her back and hissed, flicking her paw with her sharp nails out. Kit bobbed her head, chatting at Azrael as if explaining the entire ordeal.

"Enough," he shouted at the familiars.

Ibis flinched.

Selma smirked proudly. The tip of her tongue teased her lip before she turned her unreadable eyes at Ibis.

"Ostara is upon us. We do not have time for this," Azrael chastised.

Fury slowly burned in her belly. Sometimes Ibis was thankful magic was not a part of her. She would surely set her cousin's hair on fire if she could.

"Mona," Azrael barked her name harshly. "Both of you will report to Countess Isa's quarters and explain yourselves. This is unacceptable."

Regla remained quiet. Her dark eyes glanced at Tyzion and then at Ibis before lowering them to the ground. "I will explain what happened," she replied in a regretful tone.

"What? But we didn't...they attacked us," Mona hissed.

"Before or after the insults?" Azrael questioned. "Don't lie. It will not end well for you."

Mona grunted, and with a huff, she stormed out of the library, bypassing a smirking Selma.

Regla kneeled to the ground, reaching her hand out to Chaos. "*¿Perdóname?*"

Chaos meowed, barring her teeth. Before Regla stood, Sooty flew down, stretching her wings wide.

"*Hooot,*" she said, blinking her gigantic eyes. Her beak partially opened.

Ibis smiled.

"They said they will forgive you as long as you bring them treats," Tyzion confirmed.

Ibis and Regla shared a look. "I can do that," Regla softly said to Sooty, rising to her feet and retreating.

Selma crossed her arms and tilted her head, staring at Ibis.

"Well, this is a total mess," she said. Her smoky voice soothed the anger Ibis felt burning in her belly. "Need help cleaning it up?" she asked with a shove of her hip. Ibis giggled.

"You really want to set your cousin's hair on fire?" asked Azrael.

Ibis shrugged her shoulders.

"It's not nice to read people's mind," she reminded him.

"It's not nice to set people's hair on fire either," he said, "But it could be fun," he said with a wink.

Sooty hooted and Chaos meowed.

Kit swished her tail and stood on her hind legs for Tyzion to pick her up. Happily content to be in the arms of the guard, getting belly rubs.

"Holy headless horseman balls," cried out Andrew. "What happened?"

Elizabeth rushed past her brother and embraced Ibis fiercely. "Are you alright? Who are we hexing?"

Ibis relaxed, hugging her friend tightly. "I'm alright."

"No hexing," warned Azrael.

"Party-pooper," muttered Andrew, joining in on the embrace.

Elizabeth turned and faced Azrael. "What happened?"

Sooty flew down and gently landed on her shoulder. Bumping her head against Elizabeth's. She ran her fingers through Sooty's feathers. Chaos jumped up and laid across Andrew's shoulder, purring.

Ibis went over everything with them, explaining why Mona and Regla were in the library. She left out the nasty comment of turning to stone, but Sooty did not. Azrael understood the familiar, and his eyes deepened in their red glow. He must have shared his thoughts with Selma.

"That bitch," Selma hissed. "We are so setting her hair on fire."

"No one is setting anyone's hair on fire," Azrael warned.

Tyzion laughed and continued to rub Kit who lay in his arms.

Selma crossed her arms, challenging.

"You can challenge me later, mate," he warned. Azrael nodded to Tyzion, who placed Kit in Selma's arms.

"We found another familiar. I would keep her, but I think she would be better with you," his deep baritone voice spoke as he reached for the box he brought in and left hidden in the doorway.

Ibis glanced at the box. A pink nose with whiskers peaked out from the box. "She's a little squeamish, but we got her to calm down. She seemed to relax the closer we got to the library."

Ibis lifted the lid.

Staring at her, a ball of brown fur with long ears and black eyes resided within the box. Her little pink nose with long white whiskers shivered and sniffed before standing on her back hind legs. She was all fur. Brown with white on her belly. Pink paw pads. Pink nose and even the inside of her long ears were pink. The little bunny was adorable.

Ibis lifted the bunny from the box and cradled it in her arms. It remained calm, taking a deep breath, as if knowing it was safe and home. Cooing and petting the bunny, she lifted her eyes at Tyzion and smiled, and then back at Selma and Azrael.

"Where did you find it?"

Tyzion cleared his throat. "Out by the Stone Garden. We are not sure how long she's been out there. We think she's a newborn. Azrael has vetted her through. She is safe and can be kept here at The Veil."

Elizabeth ran her fingers through her fur. "She's so soft."

"Cute little rodent," Andrew said.

"She's not a rodent."

"Totally a rodent."

These two. They just can't ever agree on anything.

"A bunny is not a rodent," Ibis corrected.

"Looks like a rodent," muttered Andrew.

The once calm bunny exposed her sharp front teeth and snapped at Andrew's hand. Azrael laughed, and Tyzion chuckled. Elizabeth went over to the bunny and cooed over its little head.

"Don't listen to that ugly, mean old witch. He knows nothing about bunnies."

Selma giggled and laid her hand on Ibis's shoulder. "What are you going to name it?"

Ibis looked over at the bunny, trying to feel it's aura. Something she did with the other familiars. Something just clicked when she did that.

"Rosie," she whispered, catching the bunny close it's eyes and lean into her chest.

Selma ran her long finger over Rosie's head, down her nose. "Rosie," she repeated. "I think she likes it."

Yes. She did. Ibis felt it. How, she didn't know, but somehow she did. Ibis always did. Every time she named her familiars, she felt this overwhelming connection with them.

"Hey, what happened to Charlie?"

Wait, what?

She turned and found Andrew picking up pieces of stone from the ground and pointing up at the statue. She groaned. Elizabeth growled.

"It's Oliver," they all said.

Chapter Four

Naughty Tail

I bis used her mortar and pestle to finish grinding the stone into fine pieces, thanks to Tyzion and Azrael's help. They crushed the larger pieces for her and Andrew ground most of them till it was fine enough for her to transfer into her mortar. Once there, she created a cement mixture. Hopefully she could patch up the damaged wing on Oliver and make it look like new. Or at least make the damage look unnoticeable.

All the familiars were situated peacefully in their beds, or her bed, cocooned under covers, near the fire, sitting warm, enjoying the twinkling lights scattered around her bookshelves and the cool breeze blowing in from her open bay window. Selma found the fairy lights amusing. So much so, she added them to her bedroom as a joke. Only it backfired on her. Azrael found them adorable and instantly wanted more. He added them all over their quarters.

It wasn't easy to get to Oliver, but Ibis balanced the mortar along with the bindings and herself as she crossed onto the banister, over the ledge, and into his lap.

"Hi," she whispered, not that he ever responded, but she always felt it necessary to say hello when she sat with him. "I'm sorry about your wing. Mona," she sighed, "Mona can be such a jerk face sometimes. I hope I can fix it."

She placed the mortar on his open palm and stood on his lap, blushing. "Don't get fresh with me," she playfully warned before leaning her body over his face. She reached his wing and spread the cement mixture on the damaged area. Evenly spreading out the mixture. Adding and smoothing where it needed before wrapping the section. She would need to paint over the wrap after it dried up. But for now, this would prevent from dripping. She leaned back and dusted her hands off with the rag, holding onto his enormous shoulder and leaning back to look into his stone eyes. "See. Good as new," brilliantly smiling, placing a quick peck on his stone cheek. She glanced at the messy bandages and shrugged. "Well, sort of, but once I paint over it, no one will notice it." She laid her head on his shoulder and sighed. "Oh, maybe I could draw a tattoo on you. Something mysterious and badass, like a raven." She swayed her foot loosely back and forth, not caring that she was three levels above the ground. Then an idea hit her like an energy ball. Snapping her fingers, she pointed at Oliver, "I know, I'm going to add my initials on your wing. She grab the spatula she used to spread and with the tip, she carved into the semi-dry mixture I.M.H. and drew a heart around it.

She giggled and sat back on Oliver's lap, listening to music from her tablet and singing along to Taylor Swift's Enchanted. A wistful feeling washed over her as if phantom arms wrapped around her, snuggling her closer while she sang the lyrics. She leaned deeper into Oliver's chest, resting her head on the stone. Silently, she wished a heartbeat would thump. Sometimes she almost thought she heard it.

Wishful thinking.

The creaking sound of the library door caught her attention. She leaned to the side, peering over Oliver's stone arms.

"Are you and your boyfriend having a moment again?" Elizabeth teased.

"Don't be jealous."

"I shouldn't be," Elizabeth said with a wink, lugging a bookbag over her shoulders with her up the spiral staircase, "but he is so delish, it's hard not to be."

Ibis giggled and arched her eyebrow at the bag. "What brings you here?"

"Boredom, books, boyfriend material," she trailed off.

"And?" Ibis asked, tilting her head.

"And a minor spell, even you can pull off."

Frick frack.

"Have you been drinking Selma's Dragon Juice again?"

Elizabeth blinked. Twice. As if she had to think about it. "No, but it sounds amazing. She needs to make some for the Ostara Ball. Can you imagine?"

Actually, she couldn't. "No, not really."

Elizabeth hung her bag on one of the Oliver's horns, and squeezed in next to Ibis on his lap. "I'm sorry, Ibis. I didn't mean to bring it up."

"It's fine. It's just a dance, right? I'm sure they are pretty boring."

Elizabeth remained quiet and wrapped her arms around Ibis's shoulders. "How about I hang out with you instead? I don't need to go."

"You have to go. Who's going to watch over your brother?"

She shrugged her shoulders. "Eh, he's a big witch. He can manage on his own."

Ibis arched her eyebrow.

"Right. So maybe he needs a watchful eye. Do you think Azrael would watch him?"

That would be the day.

"Azrael would lock him up in one of those fancy bird cages he admires."

Azrael had a fascination with bird cages. The bigger, the better. People speculated that he and Selma had transformed their quarters into a giant birdcage from the inside. Canopy-bed and all. They even had a peacock as a familiar named Seraphina.

"Brothers are such pains in the vagina hole," Elizabeth muttered, leaning against Oliver's lap.

Ibis giggled. "You love your brother."

"Doesn't mean I don't think he's a pain in my vagina hole."

Sometimes she wondered what it felt like to have a sibling. Being an only child was lonely. Then again, witnessing the relationships of siblings at The Veil quickly changed her mind. Maybe being a single child wasn't so bad, even if she craved being a part of something united.

Part of a bond.

Part of a family.

It wasn't as if she didn't have a family. She did. It's just they were not close.

Not united.

Not bonded.

She wondered if she was even a part of the family. Or even wanted to be.

Sadness crept into her lonely heart.

She was content with her position in The Veil. She understood her role and her place within the Coven.

But oh, how she wished she could be a part of something more.

"Before I forget," Elizabeth said with a loud yawn, flipping around and reaching back to get her backpack. "Book and boyfriend material," she said, plopping the bag in her lap.

Goddess, the bag looked heavy.

"How many books and book boyfriends did you bring me?"

"Honey, you need options," winking with a wide smile. She opened her bag and snuggled close to Ibis, grabbing the first thick book and opening it to the tab pages. "I tabbed the pages for you. Red means spicy time. Pink is sweet. Purple is multiple..."

"Multiple what?"

"Partners," she replied saucily, wiggling her eyebrows.

Her eyes rounded.

"Just read the codes in the front of the books. I added it for you and I also put a description of the beings in the front of the books."

"Beings?"

"Well, they are not all humans. Some are Werewolves, Vampires, Dragons. You know what, just read the books." She drummed her fingers on one book. "Not this one, though."

Ibis tilted her head, biting her lip. Hiding her smile.

"I claim him," Elizabeth whispered dreamingly, hugging the book close to her heart. The book had worn edges. Multiple red tabs decorated the ends of the pages, as well as a few pink ones. There were some green and blue, something Ibis would need to look up the meaning of.

"Well, there are plenty of books here for me to read," Ibis said with a smile. "One less won't matter."

Elizabeth grinned. Not just any grinned. It was her I know something you don't know look and I'm going to rub it in your face grin.

"Good, because these beings are perfect for you. Now I personally would go with the wolf or dragon, but if you want something more mundane than Jude Hardy, also known as Crow from The Reapers, M.C. is delicious. A definite bad boy with a heart of gold and hung like a dragon shifter."

Ibis stared incredulously at her. Her hands shook as she picked up the book Elizabeth referred to. The man on the cover was heart stopping gorgeous with tattoos all along his arms. Dark hair and dark eyes with a hint of scruff on his face. A small smile tugged his lips.

"And here's the spell to bring him forward," Elizabeth casually dropped a sheet of paper on top of the cover, tapping her finger rapidly.

Ibis sucked in a deep breath. "Are you insane? I can't bring forth something or someone."

"Oh, come on. It's an easy singular spell."

"Then you do it."

"I can't. My magic has to be done with Andrew. I will not ask him to do this. Remember, pain in my vagina hole."

Ibis waved her hands in the air, dropping the book. A loud banging sound echoed throughout the library as Mr. Jude Hardy landed on the first floor. Face down. On his face.

"Fine," Elizabeth pouted. "If you don't want Hardy or any book boyfriend, then bring Oliver forward. This book has a gargoyle and he does somethings with his tail that will rock your world. Come on," she whined. "Let's find out if Oliver can do the same."

"What?!"

Elizabeth scrambled through her bag and grabbed another novel with a gargoyle on the front page. She opened a red tab and shoved it under Ibis's nose. "Read."

Ibis silently read the paragraph, not only tabbed red, but it was also highlighted in pink with a big red heart drawn around it. Heat fired up in her belly and made its way up her chest and bloomed in her cheeks. *The gargoyle used his tail to...*

Ibis's eyes rounded. She tossed the book at Elizabeth and leaned over Oliver's lap, half hanging over the ledge, with her ass in the air, ignoring her friend's annoying laughter, while she located Oliver's tail. It coiled around the column underneath him. She leaned back, completely flushed and breathless.

"That cannot be true," she whispered.

Elizabeth shrugged. "Only one way to find out," she said, holding the spell between two fingers.

She would not do this.

Ibis kept telling herself she would not do this. Even though she went to the glass pantries and collected all the ingredients. At least Elizabeth's handwriting was clear and precise. She shouldn't have any mishap with this spell.

Right?

Right.

She could do this. It was a singular spell. She didn't need a partner. Ibis could do this on her own. Besides, she was a witch.

A Light Witch.

A Heliodoro, dammit.

She could do this.

She stared at all the ingredients she laid out on the table.

Who was she kidding? She couldn't do this. She was going to blow up the library. It was bound to happen. Ibis Heliodoro, Light Witch to The Order, was going to blow up the library.

Frick frack. So be it.

She grabbed her mortar and pestle and smashed the ingredients as instructed. Reading, no double, no triple reading each line before performing the task. Once that was done, she glanced at the book laying on the floor.

Ugh! She would need to sprinkle the magic over the book.

She read the words written and rehearsed them over and over. Careful not to touch the magic dust while reading the words.

Her eyes closed. She centered herself, calming her nerves and feeling the room. Slowly, her feet moved and located what she always referred to as the magic spot for her to perform a ritual. Eyes opened, she sat back on Oliver's stone lap. Rotating her shoulders, she closed her eyes again and took multiple breaths. With steady hands, she lowered the mortar onto Oliver's opened palm. Reaching into the mortar, her fingers brushed the powder. A rush of power ignited through her arm.

She smiled. The magic was alive.

She licked her lips and breathed in deep, reciting the spell again in her mind.

With a fistful of magic dust cupped in her hands, she held it up and kneeled on Oliver's stone lap, placing a half-burned candle before her. By flicking her wrist, she caused a slow ember to ignite and rise into a full, glowing flame. Triumph bloomed in her chest. Steadying her hand, she recited the spell with crisp, coherent words.

"By this candle's light,
I ask the Goddess for her might.
To use thy magic dust provided,
And bring forth their soul guided.
A singular spell to be heard,
By the power of one to be returned."

A surge of energy flowed through her hand, heating the powder, turning it to golden

It worked!

Ibis couldn't believe it. She blew the dust from her hands, letting it fall to the ground over the book. She couldn't help but laugh and jump up and down with excitement as she watched the fading embers fall to the ground.

Wait. Why were they fading?

No.

No, they couldn't fade.

There was nothing in the spell saying it would fade. Frustrated and disappointed, she kicked the bowl in Oliver's palm and spilled the contents all over him. Some fading embers landed on his lap. She rolled her eyes and growled.

Great. Now she was going to burn down the library and Oliver with it. She sighed, completely defeated. She picked up the damaged mortar. Sooty hooted from her perch.

"I know. I know. I should have known better than to do the spell. So stupid. At least it doesn't smell."

Ibis leaned against Oliver. "I really suck as a witch. Maybe turning to stone isn't such a bad idea."

Defeated, she picked herself up and patted Oliver on the shoulder before grabbing everything around him. She swept up the remaining dust and went downstairs to clean up the mess before anyone found any traces of failed magic.

Goddess knows that was the last thing she needed right now.

Chapter Five

Seaweed Hair, Don't Care

H er voice.

There it is again. Whoever the female was, she was chatty. Often, he would hear her sing a melody or two. Other times, she chatted about random things occurring throughout her day. She read to him, which he found the most soothing of all. There was something about her that made his exile endurable. The smokiness in her tone and the melody in her voice soothed the beast in him. Well, at least it did till she mentions the hideous name given to him.

Oliver.

What name is this? Not his, that's for sure. He was not familiar with this realm, but he was sure Oliver was not a suitable name. When she called him Oliver, a slow rumble occurred in his chest. That is, it would occur if he were not stone.

Damn curses.

Damn witches.

He shouldn't feel anything for this female. From the lingering voices fluttering around, she was a witch herself. Apparently not a good one, but, none the less, he shouldn't feel this need to shield her from the others who visit.

The need to hold her when she sat in his lap and read or sang about Funky Towns overwhelmed him. This is a bizarre place. Why would a town be funky and why haven't the residents done anything about it? It made no sense.

Then there were the slightest caresses. Just a hint of a touch on his shoulder or his lap. Something he could not feel either way. Whatever spell the witches had him under was waning off. For years, he sat stoned. Never feeling and barely hearing his surroundings.

Until her.

Ibis.

The other female had said her name was Ibis.

Ibis, he repeated, letting it roll around in his mind.

She had drawn him out of the darkness into a fog.

A blinding haze.

Still, at least it was not the damning darkness.

If only he could chuckle at the nonsense conversation between Ibis and her friend. There was no such thing as a rattling tail. No creature existed. It really is a bizarre, bizarre place.

His mind drifted off, focusing back on Ibis as she spoke.

"By this candle's light,
I ask the Goddess for her might.
To use thy magic dust provided,
And bring forth their soul guided.
A singular spell to be heard,
By the power of one to be returned."

Ah, his little Ibis.

Her voice pounded in his head. The surrounding haze darkened with fury and swirled with madness. A sharp, undeniable pain shot into his temples, pulsing rapidly. Increasing with every turn, the internal tornado in his mind grew wilder. He growled deeply.

Fuck.

Pain shot through his eyes, into the back of his mind and down his spine. He fought the rage burning inside him. What did she do?

Damn curse.

Damn witches.

Before he released a roar, his eyes focused. Despite still being stone, he could make out the old library where he was captured. In his lap, sat defeated, a stunning female. Her auburn hair, full of long waves, hung down her back. She was muttering something before she stood and patted his shoulders and walked away.

His eyes lost sight of her.

Ibis.

His little Ibis.

Ibis closed the library doors and walked into the main hall. She needed fresh air and a change of scenery. The spell was an epic failure. She'd placed all the books on her nightstand and cleaned up the ashy mess she made with the ingredients. Good thing a cleaning spell was something she could perform. Maybe it was because Selma made it foolproof for her. Regardless, she'd cleaned everything up and left the familiars resting, promising them a treat when she returned.

The Order hid The Veil within the mundane world. From the outside, it would appear as an old private home with its two-story facade. Dark gray walls and even darker borders rimmed the large windows of the home. The black-shingle roof sparkled in the moonlight. Large Magnolia trees settled around the landscape, with years of moss drooping down the branches. An array of pink flowers hugged the walkway, sidewalk and porch, along with gardenias. A wrap-around porch with black rocking chairs sat peacefully while the mundane world hustled and bustled its way unknowingly.

Who knew behind the large, heavy double doors, another world existed? A world full of spells, enchantment, and otherworldly beings.

Ibis stared at the double doors, wishing for once she would leave and not return. Find a cottage somewhere outside of the small town. Settle in the far end of the forest where she could cause havoc with her faulty spells without the critical eyes of The Order or the humans.

Casting Cove was quaint.

Cute.

Small.

She loved the little town. The shops and small restaurants. Every season, the town decorated Main Street with buckets and towers of flowers. It looked like an enchanted little village. This year, The Veil gifted many of the seasonal flowers to the town. Ibis was ecstatic since she was a part of the Flower Committee. She sent Gardenias, along with Dahlias, and Tulips, and many other colorful flowers, to the town. Each season, she arranged fresh flowers to be viewed around town. It was an unwritten agreement between the mundane and The Veil. One that had been in place for longer than many witches remembered. After all, witches lived quite a long time.

Ibis lingered by the great doors a little longer before she turned with a heavy sigh and made her way towards the Duo Quarters. Many paired witches lived in this hallway. Elizabeth and Andrew were among them. So were Selma and Azrael and unfortunately, Mona and Regla. She sneered just thinking about them. It was a good thing Elizabeth and Andrew's quarters were in the front, something they hated. It was Selma's request to place them there. Ibis learned later it was for her benefit. Easier for her to sneak in if she ever needed to.

Another reason she adored Selma.

Ibis could visit the Duo Quarters. Of course witches could visit and mingle with one another. However, it was imperative paired witches returned to their quarters and remained together overnight.

According to rumor, if paired witches were not in their quarters while resting, someone could syphon their magic, leaving their pairing weak. People said that this only happened once but never at The Veil.

It was the reason the strict rules were in place for visitors to not stay overnight, and it was a rule she followed.

Always.

Knocking on their door, she waited patiently, nodding as fellow witches walked past. She knocked once more, a little louder, leaning against the door. Mumbled sounds and a deep grumble made her pause. That did not sound like Andrew.

She reached for the handle and stepped forward. A little splash at her feet caused her to pause. Why was there water seeping from the doorway?

Frick frack. What trouble did the twins get into this time?

The door pushed opened and Elizabeth rushed out. Her soaked blond and pink hair stuck to her face wildly. Mascara smeared under her dark brown eyes.

"What is going on?" Ibis whispered, careful not to draw attention. Not that it would be hard considering the state Elizabeth was in and the pool of water leaking from her doorway.

Elizabeth squealed like a crazed banshee, jumping up and down in the water before grabbing Ibis by her elbow and shoving her inside. The room wreaked of murky sea water. Green plants plastered against the walls and floors. Water flooded their living space.

"It worked!" shouted Elizabeth with glee. She wiped her hair away from her face. Small green particles collected around her forehead and embedded in her hair. "You did it. Right? It was you. I mean. It had to be you. No one else knows about the spell except you," she rambled on, jumping and spinning around. "I can't believe you did it," she said, twirling round and round, splashing water with her feet.

Ibis wiped her face. She licked her lips. The salty taste confused her. Sea water.

She reached over and plucked a green particle from Elizabeth's hair, rubbing it between her fingers.

Seaweed.

Elizabeth bit her lip, shuffling her feet back and forth. Her excitement was on the verge of bursting out.

"What worked?"

She let out another squeal. "Come,' dragging Ibis into her private room. "Remember, he is mine."

Ibis stated, confused. "What are you talking- "

The door opened, cutting Ibis off, leaving her speechless.

It couldn't be.

The book Elizabeth took with her was wide open. Pages swayed back and forth while a fountain of sea water funneled out. Seaweed seeped through from the pages, landing next to a man. A very large. Very tall. Very devilish handsome man.

Frick fucking frack.

"You should have seen him when he came out of the pages. He had his Mer-tail. He shifted to human. I had to let him borrower Andrew's clothes, but as you can see, he's a lot bigger than Andrew. A lot bigger," Elizabeth giggled and then sighed.

"He's a- "

"Merman. Yup. So hot," she said in a low tone, stepping in front of Ibis and making her way to the Merman. "This is Ronan, captain of the Atillians," she said proudly.

Ronan stepped silently forward. His human-like features were sharp and pronounced, from his jawline to his high cheekbones. Golden eyes shined unconventionally against his light, ash-like skin. Small, speckled, golden scales scattered around his forehead, down his jawline and further down his neck. Dark, wavy, brown hair hung down to his shoulders.

Ibis extended her hand. "Hi," she mumbled. "Ronan, is it? Welcome to, uh, well, welcome to the Veil."

His large golden eyes blinked, and his head tilted as he stared at her hand. He glanced back at Elizabeth, who smiled encouragingly. He reached out and grabbed her hand. His scaly hands were smoother than she expected.

Warm.

Then it hit her. Like an electric bolt, supercharged with a trippy concoction only a badass witch could handle the next morning.

"Wait. You mean the spell worked?"

Elizabeth jumped up and down, clapping obnoxiously. "Yes. Isn't he grand?" She sighed, leaning her head against Ronan's broad arms, since she barely reached his shoulders.

"I don't know what is going on, but I must return to Atillia. My command needs me." His melodic voice captivated them both.

Ibis chewed her lip. Well, that might be a problem.

Elizabeth frowned. "What's another day?" she asked hopeful.

The back of his hand gently caressed Elizabeth's cheek. "My pearl, if there is a way for me to stay and discover more of you, I would."

Elizabeth leaned into his hand, and Ibis rolled her eyes. She might as well have hearts swirling around her head.

"I'll find my way back to you," he whispered to her as if Ibis was not standing there watching the exchange. He leaned forward and captured Elizabeth in a deep kiss, wrapping her in his arms and lifting her off the ground.

Goddess.

Get a room, Ibis thought to herself.

Wait.

They are in a room.

She needed to get out of the room.

Ibis turned her gaze away and plucked at the seaweed on the wall, collecting it from the table and cleaning up the common area, while Elizabeth continued passionately kissing her book boyfriend as if he were the last drop of sea water left in the world. He slowly released her to the ground, before placing one more soft kiss on her forehead and whispering something private to her. His golden eyes glowed, as did his markings on his forearms, before he removed his borrowed clothes and jumped into the funnel of water gushing from the book.

Elizabeth sighed and her shoulders slumped before she jumped and spun around. Her eyes bulged.

Ibis dropped the seaweed from her hands and glanced at the door and then back at Elizabeth before they both yelled, "The library!"

Chapter Six
The Library

D amn curses.

Damn witches.

Oliver stood up straight for the first time in over a century. For a gargoyle, he was still a youngling in their standards. But right now, every bone and muscle cracked and ached. Standing over seven feet tall, he was one of the tallest of his kind. Guardians had to be in order to invoke fear in others. That was why villagers and townspeople sought them for protection against outsiders and miscreants.

He looked around the library, sniffing the unusual scents. He recalled his encounter with the witches and snarled at the very memory of them. Most times, gargoyles were nomads and traveled alone. They typically only returned to their birth colony, for one thing.

To mate.

But he did not recall any of this. Try as he might, he could remember nothing before the voices.

Their voices.

Everything was blank. None of it made sense. It felt as if he went from non-existence to existing. Somewhere in the darkness, he could hear them. A repetitive chanting. Over and over.

Bright blue hazy lights blinded his vision. His muscles stretched and pulled, breaking loose from some tight hold he was not aware he was under. His legs raised him up and over, rising above a flimsy paper-like ledge. Finally breaking through the entrance, his wings expanded and thrust through the opening, releasing a loud roar.

Without warning, the blue lights vanished, and they flung him onto a hard floor. Candlelight flickered around the room full of strange artifacts and pages with drawings on them. The book laid open before him, flapping its pages back and forth.

"We did it," said a soft-spoken voice.

"¿Y ahora qué?"

"Well, we wait and ask him for his help."

With shaky legs, he slowly rose to his feet. His head snapped up and bared his teeth in warning. His violet eyes glowed as he stretched his wings, taking up most of the room before leaping above over their heads to a ledge high above them, crouching down. He wobbled to the right and caught himself before falling. Disoriented and confused, he scanned the room for a way out.

"Why have you summoned me?" he demanded in a hoarse voice, his long tail swished and snapped loudly against the stone pillars.

"Silence! You will speak when spoken to and show respect to the Light witches of the Order."

He glared at them. His eyes searched his surroundings.

"He is still weak and disoriented. We can syphon his strength. Use it for The Veil Force in training."

"No," said the soft-spoken one. "That is not what we agreed on."

His eyes flared.

He hissed and stretched his hand out, releasing his sheathed claws. His tail twirled around the column beneath him. He would tear it from the ground and use it if need be. They dare to threaten him?

A bolt of light shot at his head. He dodged it and roared at them.

"Recite the spell. ¡Ahora!"

"No. I will not. This is not what we agreed on. We agreed to ask him to be our guardian. To help us train The Veil Force. Not steal his strength. I will not curse him into stone-sleep," the soft-spoken one said.

"Then I will do it myself."

A pounding ache echoed in his brain as the witch held her hand up and snapped her wrist, reciting her chant. He froze, unable to move from his spot.

What was happening to him?

His heart raced as a chill ran down his spine, and his limbs iced over. She was forcing him to stone.

No!

He tried moving his arms, his legs, anything to fight the curse, and nothing worked. The curse trapped him.

His palm turned up right as it froze. His eyes glared at the witches before darkness engulfed the ray of light in his eyes.

Unfrozen and yet still cold, his body shook and ached. He flexed his hands.

Open and close.

Open and close.

Open and close.

He then unsheathed his claws and winced. He did it again and again till the ache dulled away. His tail remained coiled in place. He growled.

Reaching for it, he worked the muscles and aches. He hoped it would not remain curled.

He bent over and stretched his back and then leaned back, popping more bones and groaning. A sudden hoot snapped his head to the right. He blinked and stared at the feathered creature.

"What are you?" His voice was rough. Rougher than he had ever heard. Low and groveling. He cleared his throat and leaned in to sniff the little beast. It made another hooting sound before it flapped its wings and stepped back.

"Owl?" he said. "You're Sooty," he whispered, remembering Ibis speaking of her familiars, as she referred to them. "Who is Fox?"

Kit released a raspy bark followed by a series of whines and shrieks.

"I see," Oliver said. "You are a fox, but your name is Kit. Understood." He rubbed her forehead. A soft smile tugged his lips as the little critter's eyes closed. Something soft and noisy kneaded his leg. Short spotted fur twisted around his lower leg, bumping her head and meowing. Yellow peering eyes glowed, beckoning to be picked up. "I presume you must be Chaos. I overheard a few stories about you, little deviant," he cooed, running his long fingers through soft fur. Chaos clutched her claws into his tattered clothing and climbed her way up, jumping onto Oliver's shoulders and curling around his neck. She sat there content, kneading her claws into one shoulder.

Oliver flexed his hands again and stretched his back, groaning from both pain and relief. His eyes roamed the strange chamber, something he could not do before. Bizarre relics, bottles, and bound scrolls filled the room. He'd seen nothing like it before.

Strange place.

Curious, he glanced around and sniffed the air. A sweetness like he never smelled before filled his nostrils. He peered around the smaller room. Soft embers glowed from the sconces on the walls. Underneath was an unmade cot with layers of blankets. A small brown bundle of fur lay in the center. Its pink nose twitched and head tilted before burying itself underneath the blankets. Oliver chuckled and ignored the newcomer.

The scent grew stronger as he neared the cot. Piles of bound scrolls sat high on the floor. Others were placed on shelves all against the wall, high to the ceiling.

Sooty hooted and flapped her wings.

He snapped his head and swung around, bumping into the piles, causing them to tumble with his wings and tail. Pain ricochet down his nerves into his arms from his wing. He released a loud growl and stretched his wing before growling again at the damage he had not seen before.

He folded his wing in and ran his hand over the bandage. Some sort of picture was carved into his skin. He couldn't make out what it said. Unsure, he sneered at the sting and turned back to the noise he heard.

His ears twitched as someone made their way into the chamber. The door creaked open. A powerful scent filled the room.

Unfamiliar.

Enchanted.

Masculine.

"Ibis?" the male voice called out into the calm silence. "Where is she?"

Chaos mewled from Oliver's shoulder and hissed while Kit bared her little sharp teeth. With silent steps, he lowered himself into the shadows and crouched on his original perch. It wasn't till the door opened again and the sweet scent flooded his senses. He knew his little one had returned.

Frick frack toad's tongue. This cannot be happening. It just cannot be happening. She was happy the spell worked, but why did it work on Elizabeth's book?

"Who did you choose?" Elizabeth said while skipping down the hallway. Not caring at the unusual stares she received from the wet hair or seaweed stuck in it. Or for leaving a salt water trail all the way down the hall to the library.

"It didn't work." Ibis said through clenched teeth as she walked then sped up to a slight jog.

Frick frack.

Frick frack.

FRICK FRACK!

Finally she ran the rest of the way, uncaring who saw her, and ignored the wet sloshing noises coming from Elizabeth's shoes. She ignored the unusual stares from passerbys. She ignored Selma's stare. She especially ignored Elizabeth's giggles as they reached the library, which was open.

Open?

She closed the door. Ibis was sure of it.

They stopped outside of the door.

"Did you - "

"No, I closed the door before I came to see you."

"Do you - "

"It didn't work. I'm telling you, Elizabeth, it didn't work. No one popped out of a book," Ibis said, waving her hands.

"Maybe he - "

"It didn't work," she hissed and peered into the crack door. Elizabeth squeezed her wet head underneath and let out a gasp.

A very loud gasp.

Ibis reached over and placed a hand over Elizabeth's mouth, yanking her back away from the door before the shadow of a man could see them. Ibis couldn't believe it. Her eyes had to be playing tricks on her. But they couldn't be. Elizabeth saw the same.

In the library, standing where the book landed earlier, stood a shadow.

A man.

But who? There was no book near him. Could it be this *Jude Hardy* character?

Elizabeth reached over and yanked her hand away. "It's him," she squealed, pretending to swoon and wiggled her eyebrows. She tilted her head, encouraging Ibis to go in.

Ibis shook her head and mouthed, "No way."

Elizabeth mouthed back, "Yes way."

Ibis rolled her eyes, and Elizabeth flicked her nipple.

Hard.

Ibis hissed. "What is wrong with you?"

Elizabeth wiggled her brows again. "He will make you feel better. Now go."

She was going to set Elizabeth's hair on fire. How? She didn't know, but she would figure it out. Taking a deep breath, she rubbed her sore breast before swallowing the lump of nerves and pushed open the library door. She entered, pretending not to hear Elizabeth's squishy footsteps behind her, sneaking in and hiding.

The shadow turned, making his way towards her.

Uneasiness crept in. She knew that walk. The light brought her secret shadow man out of darkness.

Elton Salas.

The Elton her *Tia* had paired her with for a mate. The same Elton she denied.

That Elton was in her library unannounced and uninvited.

"There you are," he said in his casual, smooth voice.

"What are you doing here?"

"Just visiting," he said with a shrug, as if it was a normal occurrence.

"The library was closed, and I was not here. Why would you enter uninvited?"

He laughed. "Why would I require an invitation? After all, you and I are engaged at this point."

She stared at him, dumbfounded. He cannot be serious.

"Elton, I was very clear on the matter of our pairing. I did not accept the match. Which means I will not mate with you. Which also means there is no betrothed, engagement, commitment or whatever else you have conjuring up in that head of yours."

He could not be that obtuse.

Could he?

He smiled.

Not just any smile.

A smile that made every hair on her body rise with acute awareness and every nerve stand alert. A smile that set her on edge. A smile meant to scare and not entice.

"You will be mine, Ibis Heliodoro," he said in a low, slithering voice. A voice she had not heard from him before. It chilled her skin. She stood still when he closed the distance and leaned in to whisper, "You will learn your place."

Insufferable man.

Learn her place? Oh, how she wished she could snap her fingers and turn the wretched, vile snake of a man into a toad.

No. Not a toad. Toads were great familiars. A worm. A slimy, muddy worm, slinking his way through the dirt, hiding his existence from ferocious predators like a bluebird or a Wren.

Her lips raised in a sneer, and a loud growl erupted the silence in the library. Her hand flew to her mouth. That growl was not hers.

Wait. Was it?

No. She was pretty sure it wasn't.

Elton pulled back, surprised. His perfectly tweezed eyebrow arched mockingly at her. Before he could comment, the growl came again, louder this time. Her eyes grew wider, as did his. Elton turned and reached for her hand.

She smacked it away and distanced herself from him, backing away from his advances. She wished the snapping finger magic would work right about now. An ominous shadow cast wide on the ground. Suddenly, it landed in front of her, shielding her. It stood tall and broad. Wings spread wide against rippling muscles on stone like skin. Eyes glanced over its shoulders, illuminating in violet orbs before turning its gaze back. Ibis scooted back and then stopped with a gasp. Her eyes catching sight of a bandaged wing. A bandage she had placed.

Oliver!

Chapter Seven
Nothing To See Here

Three things were for certain.

First, Oliver was huge. Like huge, huge. Tall, broad shoulders, wings took up the entire center before colliding with the columns on either side. His curled tail snapped against the floor. Funny, she never imagined his tail would be curled. Something about that made her heart warm and fuzzy.

Wait. What? No. No warm and fuzzy feelings allowed.

Stop it.

Second, he was alive. As in, breathing the same oxygen, walking around her library, staring at her with glowing violet eyes.

Violet eyes!

Goddess. Of all colors, she had not expected that. Well, she didn't expect him to be walking, breathing, growling around her library either, but one crisis at a time.

Oh, and his tail did not seem to vibrate. Not that this bit of information was of any importance.

She was in so much trouble.

So, so, so much trouble. She couldn't wait till she got her hands on Elizabeth. Where was she, anyway? The loud roar jarred her from her thoughts. Elton squeaked and jumped back. If Oliver kept this up, the entire Veil would be on alert. Without hesitating, she rounded Oliver and placed a hand against his chest.

A very warm, very hard beating chest. In his crouched position, she could reach him. His gaze turned to her, losing their angry glow. He tilted his head, staring at her. She swallowed a nervous knot in throat.

A loud thunk came from behind her. Oliver's wing shielded her from whoever the assailant was. She peaked over and found Elizabeth holding a watering can over Elton's body.

"What did you do?" Ibis asked.

"I barely touched him," Elizabeth whispered, looking at the watering can and then over Elton. "He'll be fine," her shoulders shrugged as she placed the weapon of choice on the ground and slid it with her leg behind a column. "Might just have a slight headache when he wakes. Nothing a little tea and an ache-away spell can't cure."

Oliver produced a noise that she could only describe as a chuckle, or at least she thought it was a chuckle. No sooner had Elizabeth *The Wielding Water Can Extraordinaire* made her assault, Sooty flew down and perched herself on Oliver's shoulder, followed by Kit, Rosie and Chaos. They remained close to Oliver, hiding behind his large legs. He swept them up with one hand, securing Kit and Rosie in his embrace while Chaos laid comfortably on his shoulder.

She was stunned. It was as if they have known him their entire lives. Well, technically, they knew him. Well, not knew him, knew him. But they knew of him. He lived in the damn library for frick frack sakes.

Frick frack!

She was in so much trouble. As if sensing her distress, his wing came around her shoulder and his already curled tail curled even more around her waist snuggly. Elizabeth squealed and ran to her, running her hand over the end of Oliver's tail and feeling its softness.

"Do you think it - "

"No!" Ibis shouted loudly and then placed a hand over her mouth before turning to look at Oliver. His eyes glowed brightly. A small smile tugged his full lips. "It's fine. Everything is fine," she kept telling herself, attempting to unravel her body from the cozy tail embrace and distance herself from him, slapping Elizabeth's hand off of the furry end. "We need a plan and an explanation."

"Damn right," Andrew grumbled from the doorway, shoving it open. His hands flew up and down, splashing water everywhere. Water drenched his clothes. Behind him, Ronan followed closely. "Someone wants to explain why I have a merman flooding my quar..." he froze and eyes bulged. "Jupiter's balls! Charlie is alive!"

Ibis groaned.

"You came back." Within seconds, Elizabeth launched herself into Ronan's arms, who cradled her gently while Andrew stared at them weirdly. Then back at Oliver, then back at them again.

"What did you do?" he asked Elizabeth.

Elizabeth continued to stare lovingly into Ronan's eye and waved a hand, disregarding him. "I did nothing," she said in a daze.

Andrew took two steps towards her, but someone immediately stopped him. Ronan turned, placing Elizabeth protectively behind his back. The gold flecks of scale on his skin illuminated as he posed threatening. Andrew raised two hands up and backed away slowly. "Call him off, Elizabeth," he warned in a quiet tone.

Ibis reached for Andrew, only to be blocked by a massive wing. She tried to persuade Oliver to let her pass. Instead, a deep frown and a stubborn glare met her.

Elizabeth placed a calming hand on Ronan's arm and pulled him back, easing the tension. "Easy," she said calmly. "He's not a threat. Just a pain in the vagina hole."

Ronan sneered. His golden scales glowed brighter.

"Not helping," Andrew snapped, taking another step back.

"You caused her pain," Ronan snarled. "Now, I cause you pain." He launched himself towards Andrew, catching nothing but empty air. Andrew dodged him and circled around Oliver. Not thinking twice, he barricaded himself with Ibis within Oliver's wings.

"First things first, Fish-man," he said in an elevated tone. "She's my sister. Anything to do with her vag..." Andrew gagged and covered his mouth, "with her vag..." Gagging again, he held up a finger and paled. "Anything to do with her parts is gross," he said, coughing.

Ibis pinched her nose. Could this get any worse?

"Besides," he said, waving his hands between the two of them and then glaring as Elizabeth smiled. "I don't cause her any pain. Elizabeth, call him off," he urged again, ignoring the sudden low menacing guttural sounds coming from behind him.

Ibis glanced up at Oliver's lit eyes. She placed a hand on his chest and soothed the inner turmoil brewing within him. He glanced down. Eyes dimming to a lavender hue. A soft rumble quaked his chest under her hand. Warmth spread across her cheek. Was she blushing?

Really Ibis? Get it together. This is not the time to be a blushing witch.

Ronan muttered something under his breath. Something only Elizabeth found hilarious and outright laughed. Andrew fumed.

Poor Andrew.

He was soaked to the bone and clueless.

With determination, Ibis escaped Oliver's security and stood between Ronan and him. "Everyone needs to calm down," she said with more authority, more confidence than she felt. "None of this is helping the situation."

"Exactly," cheered Andrew from behind his barricade.

A low moan and rustle came from behind them. All eyes turned to find Elton stirring. He sat up slowly and rubbed the back of head. "What happened?" he grumbled lowly, wincing at the obvious knot forming in his head. Becoming more alert, his eyes wandered around and landed on all of them and then focused solely on Ibis.

"You," he said is a sinister voice. "You will pay for this."

Ibis rounded her eyes, hands raised to stop her familiar. "Sooty," she called out right before her little devious owl swooped up the menacing watering can and flew right into Elton's head again. With a loud thunk, the tin can made contact.

Hard.

Elton's eyes rolled backwards, and he fell to his side.

"Yeah, he's going to have a headache for sure," Elizabeth whispered as she stood next to Ibis.

Frick frack.

Oliver sat quietly and observed. From the information he gathered from Sooty, Ibis performed a spell, and it worked. Not as she planned, but better than she expected to say the least. Sooty let him know Ibis was a sweet witch, with a heart of gold, but very clumsy, with poor magical skills. As it was, spells were not her thing and all the familiars seemed in agreement.

He listened as Sooty, Kit and Chaos chattered and brought him current with where he was, what the chamber was called, who the witches were and what spell brought him back from the darkness. Rosie seemed content to just lay in his arms. The little, long-eared bunny was a silent critter. Kept her opinions to herself and gazed upon Ibis.

Occasionally, Ibis would glance over at Oliver. Bright colors would stain her cheeks before turning her gaze away. Her hands fidgeted with her unruly red waves. She eased his beast. Something he had not felt before and it unsettled him.

He shouldn't feel this calm around her. He shouldn't feel the need to shield her. He shouldn't feel this ache to have her close again. He released a low grumble and swished his curled tail. He shouldn't feel anything. He should look for his way out. Which wasn't difficult to find since he spied the blue haze from the arches when he awoke. He wasn't sure if that was his way out, but he would take it, if it meant leaving behind this world.

He placed Rosie on the ground, ignoring her questioning stare. He ignored Sooty's warning, Kit's whining and Chaos attitude. It did not matter what they were saying to him. This was not his world. He was now awakened from the blasted curse bestowed on him. He would not dally with some fanciful notion of Ibis.

Bottom line, she was a witch.

Didn't matter if her voice kept him warm in the icy darkness.

Or that her nearness, even if he could not feel her, soothed his raging soul.

Not to mention, she left him longing for something more.

Something permanent.

He cursed, drawing attention from the witches, including Ibis before leaping from where he stood and flying across the railing, gliding across the center down to the arch. His eyes pierced the blue swirling depths of the haze. Nothing appeared on the other side. Would it lead him back home, or would he enter another dimension? Was this even where he came from?

Why could he not remember?

He peered over the edge. Cold water flowed into an abyss, releasing a frigid mist. A warning voice whispered in his head to wait. To seek answers. Soft footsteps glided to a stop behind him. Every nerve fired in awareness. His eyes glowed as he glanced back.

"I've never been this close to the mist," Ibis whispered, stepping closer till she stood next to him.

That surprised him.

"Are you... I mean... do you know where the misty river flows to?" Her eyes sparkled in wonderment as her muttered words disappeared into the water's lullaby. Her hand reached out to touch the water's flow. Before a drop landed on her fingers, Oliver reached out and pulled her hand back, ignoring the gasps from behind him.

"It is not safe to touch the water, little one."

He wasn't sure how or why, but there was a powerful pull coming from the mist. He didn't like it. Not one bit.

She blinked, as if coming out of a trance. His wing came forward and blocked the hypnotic lights of the blue misty water. She blinked again and shivered. A crease formed between his brows. He pulled her closer to his protection, providing her warmth. "I've seen the blue haze. It was a long time ago," he mumbled. "I'm not sure how or why I saw it, but it was there when I arrived."

Her warm, dark eyes rounded. "Here? As in here, here. Here in the library?"

"Jupiter's balls," Andrew grumbled.

"When was this?" Elizabeth asked.

Oliver's eyes roamed the room. It was quite different back then. Not as many scrolls and tomes as they had now or artifacts. Definitely no living quarters on the upper floors. That's a memory he would remember since they cursed him there.

"I vaguely remember the arch being here, along with a few columns. I do not remember there being anything on the upper floors," he frowned, recalling the memory.

Ibis placed a hand on her heart.

"But that was years ago."

He remained quiet.

"As in over..." Andrew muttered, using his fingers to count, "...forever ago."

Oliver grunted, eyes cast low to the ground, inhaling a deep breath and releasing it. A cold despair shadowed his lonely soul. It felt as if it was forever ago.

Too long ago.

"Did you come through the mist?" Ibis asked.

He stared at the waters. How could something sparkling, beautiful, and magnificent be treacherous? There was something there. Something not right in the blue haze. Lost in thought, he recounted his arrival. Sudden anger lit his eyes.

Damn curses.

Damn witches.

"Whatever enchantment they unleashed that night summoned me. It was as if I suddenly existed and came forward," he hissed. No doubt his eyes glowed.

"I don't understand. You're telling me someone has used the Bring Forth spell before? It makes little sense."

Sense? Nothing made sense.

"Little one, none of this makes sense," he grumbled, attempting to hold back his anger from her. It was not her fault for the predicament he was in. She was not even around when it happened. None of them were. From the looks of it, they were all younglings.

"Do you think the mist is your way back?" she asked.

He contemplated the same thought over and over. Why hadn't he done it already? It was the perfect opportunity for him to leave.

Escape.

Return home. But what about home? He didn't recall having a home or where home was. Even if he contemplated risking crossing the mist, what was stopping him?

You know what's stopping you.

He muttered a curse. Ibis raised her perfect eyebrows. Confusion clear in her eyes.

His wings twitched. As if testing himself, they stretched out on their accord, readying for flight. He stepped forward. Inching towards the edge of the abyss. Mist covering his foot.

"It will not let him return," pronounced Ronan with a harden voice.

"But he was here already. Maybe the spell will not affect him," Elizabeth reminded everyone.

"Spell?"

Oliver ignored Andrew's question. His mind reeling. Would the spell prevent him from returning?

Sooty landed on his shoulder, hooting and flapping her wings. He acknowledged her concerns and the others as they came close to him. Chaos jumped and slung herself around his other shoulder while Rosie made herself into a small ball on his foot. Kit leaned against his leg, her eyes wide and glossy as she stared at him.

He huffed and flapped his wings in one big swoop, creating a swoosh of air to blow into the dense mist. Barely creating a dent in its mass.

"But everyone will know something went wrong," Ibis said.

"Who's going to know?" Elizabeth challenged.

Andrew tossed his hands up at Elizabeth while Ibis stomped to the middle of the room. She pointed to the ledge where he once sat stoned, now empty. "You don't think someone is going to notice the missing giant gargoyle in the room?" Ibis asked, exasperated.

Elizabeth shrugged her shoulders. "I think we can pull this off. Everyone is going to be busy with the Ostara Ball."

Andrew groaned and stopped short.

On the ground, Elton lay on the floor. Except this time, Ibis had provided the poor sap with a pillow and blanket. Sooty reminded Oliver that Ibis had a tender heart, even though Oliver was not pleased with how she took care of Elton. Even if the man was a dick. It still stumped Oliver why Sooty referred to the man as a male's appendage.

Rosie jumped over to Elton and landed on his chest, stomping her foot while Sooty flew and grabbed the dangerous tin can, hovering over the human. Oliver made a mental note to research more on the perilous weapon. Before Sooty could clock him again over the head, Elton groaned once more and settled on the floor.

Everyone remained quiet.

Silence had never seemed so loud.

Oliver wasn't even sure if they were breathing. He turned his eyes and landed on Ibis. She still pointed towards the ledge where he once sat. Her breathing was shallow and slow. Andrew released a rush of air before he turned on Elizabeth and Ronan.

"This is madness. Everyone is going to know Charlie is missing."

Without thinking, he turned away from the mist. Away from the Arch. Away from his chance to escape, possibly. Eyes glowing, he stood straight, tall and cast a shadow over them all.

"My name is Oliver."

Chapter Eight
Ache In The Head

S he was in so much trouble. Bigger trouble than the minor mishap earlier in the day. Even bigger than denying the match with Elton. So much trouble. Ibis did something she had not done since she was a little girl. She bit her nails. Not just nibble and stop.

Oh no.

She took her nail to the edge of the skin and then moved on to the next one. What was she going to do? What was she thinking? Better yet, what the frick frack was she going to do?

Maybe Elizabeth was right. It's not as if anyone walked into the library and struck a conversation with Oliver or even greeted him. No one ever paid attention to him. Most times, witches would walk in, grab whatever they needed and return those not needed with hardly a look towards the upper levels where Oliver sat. Everything should be fine.

Right?

Of course not! What is in the world was she thinking? Nothing is going to be fine. She just performed a Bring Forth spell - which worked - only too well and released not only Mr. I Can't Keep My Fins, Hands and Come-Hither Eyes Off Of Elizabeth, but she also brought forth Oliver. Whom she thought this entire time was a statue. A real statue.

This stinks worse than a troll's ass. Panic quickly set in as she moved on to her third fingernail. Pretty soon, not only was she going to be out of nails, but she was going to leave a trail on the library floor from all the pacing.

"My name is Oliver," he pronounced each word clearly.

Precisely.

With intent.

She felt it in her core. The little butterflies swirled around her belly again, warming her insides.

No.

No swirls.

No warm feels.

They needed to stop that. She was having a crisis, and there was no time to have the warm and cozy feelings.

As if the little butterflies in her belly conjured up their own version of warm and cozy, something soft wrapped around her waist. She blinked once and then again as Oliver's tail pulled her into the envelope of his wings. His large hand came up and pulled hers away from her lips, turning it over and brushing his fingers over them.

Damn those lavender hues. She was a sucker for the color purple.

"I will stay."

Her eyes snapped up, stared into his. Words escaped her. Her brain completely went blank and then was overloaded with thoughts.

"You can't...I mean...you should at least try to return," she encouraged, trying to swallow the lump that suddenly formed in her throat. "It's not fair for you to stay. You're free now."

"But at what cost, little one?"

71

That was the problem. She needed to first find out the reason Oliver was enchanted and then trapped. Then she needed to figure out a way to silence Elton. Oh, and she had to return Mr. I'm About To Fornicate With Your B.F.F. In Front Of Everyone, merman back to his book, which was going to piss off Elizabeth. Andrew's life would become miserable. Which then pisses off Andrew. Which means she will piss off both of her best friends.

Jupiter's hairy balls. Why did this happen to her?

Elton stirred again on the floor, and she groaned. He rose from his unexpected slumber again, only for Sooty to fly right by him with the watering can and smack him across the head, knocking him over on the other side. Ibis did not care if the miserable man woke up with thirteen knots in his head and a raging, splitting headache. The idiot deserved it.

A smile tugged Oliver's lip. Something she found endearing, and then she froze.

They all did.

Before she knew what was happening, Oliver moved faster than she expected and grabbed Elton from the ground, flying him past the second floor and onto the third. Practically tossing him over the rail onto the floor. With a heavy grunt and another moan, Elton landed and remained quiet. Oliver glided down to his normal position and sat down. He expanded his wings and extended his hand. He glanced at Ibis and nodded towards the door. Her familiars scattered and raced up the stairwell. He closed his eyes to avoid the violet glows to show and hid his curled tail by his feet.

Ibis looked at Elizabeth. "Hide him," she hissed, annoyed by their lost gaze, reminiscent of star-crossed lovers.

Andrew rolled his eyes and sat down behind her desk as if it was absolutely normal for him to be there at this late hour. Elizabeth shoved Ronan between the stairwell and the book column and hurried back to the center, collecting the watering can along the way. Ibis grimaced as Andrew whistled a horrible tune.

It wasn't long before the library doors pushed open and Selma walked in with Seraphina, her peahen familiar. She was a radiant creature with brown and white feathers. A few turquoise and green eyelets blended within the whites of her long magical tail.

Selma glanced around. Her eyes remained stoic and curious. "Is everything alright here?" she asked, tilting her head to the side with an arched eyebrow.

She knows. She knows. She knows.

Ibis took a deep breath and smiled, expanding her hands. "Of course," she said in a high pitch voice. Higher than normal. So high, it cracked, causing Andrew to cough and Elizabeth's smile to wobble. "Nothing to see here."

Goddess. Please shut me up.

Selma bit the tip of her tongue and looked around the library. "Nothing to see. Interesting," she acknowledged, placing both her beautifully manicured hands behind her back. She slowly walked with long strides toward the center before nodding to Seraphina. In an instance, Seraphina shuffled and fanned out her tail. All the eyelets on her feathers opened, providing her with the gift of sight. Like a radar, she scanned the library and stopped as she reached Oliver. Selma must not have noticed. She walked towards Andrew and brushed a loose strand of hair from his forehead, pulling a piece of seaweed.

"What did you do?" she asked between clenched teeth.

Andrew's eyes grew large. He placed his hand over his heart and gasped. As if offended by the accusation. "Me? I did nothing."

Selma turned and stared at Ibis, then sliced her eyes to Elizabeth. "You."

Elizabeth sucked her bottom lip.

"What did you do? Better yet, what did you drag Ibis into?"

Ibis sighed, and Elizabeth tossed her wet hands up, splashing Selma in the face. "What makes you think I did anything?"

Selma licked her lips and shook her head. "Salt." she wiped the rest from under her eyes and rubbed the seaweed she still held in her hands from Andrew. She pointed between the two of them. "You will both report to the Azrael."

Ibis nodded, a sense of dread filling her stomach.

Andrew stood up from behind the chair and raked his fingers through his hair. Elizabeth crossed her arms defiantly. "We did nothing," he cried out.

"Someone did," Selma hissed, pulling from her cross bag a book wrapped in binding rope. "I had to bind the book. Do you know why?"

Elizabeth went to speak, and Selma held her hand up, silencing her. "Because the contents inside flew off the pages. Off the pages," she hissed again. "My quarter is full of monarch butterflies."

"You read books on butterflies?" Andrew asked incredulously.

"Lame," Elizabeth said with an exaggerated eye roll and sigh.

Selma's eyes glowed. It wasn't often Ibis witnessed Selma lose her composure, but when she did, she was a force to be reckoned with. Seraphina sensed her human distress. "Ibis, you are five seconds away from gaining two toads as your familiars."

Elizabeth gagged, and Andrew swallowed hard. "At least make me a cute tree frog," he muttered before dodging the book Selma held in her hands. The bindings came undone from the impact and fell. Pages fluttered and one by one, beautiful monarchs flew out of the book. Ibis ran over and closed the book, rebinding it and placing it securely in her desk drawer. She looked around at all the butterflies that had escaped and groaned.

She was in so much trouble.

"Oh, you do not know the world of trouble you are in," Selma confirmed. "Now explain what happened."

Before Ibis could confess, Elton awoke with a cry. He swung his arms around, attempting to scare off the butterflies flying around him as he made his way down the spiral staircase. Breathing hard and rubbing the back of his head, he stared at Ibis. "You," he growled fiercely.

Selma glared at Elton. "Why is he here?"

Where's the watering can when she needed it?

"Why don't you ask her about the assault?"

Selma glanced between Elton and Ibis. She raised her hand and pointed to Andrew and Elizabeth. "Do not move," then Selma turned her attention back to Ibis. "What assault?"

"She was.."

"I did not ask you," Selma snapped, silencing him. A low rumble came from behind them, causing Selma to turn her gaze behind them. Her eyes rounded large. Ibis turned and followed Selma's gaze. From the upper ledge, Oliver snapped his tail and opened his eyes. Purple hues glowed back down at them as he tilted his head.

A smirk teased his full lips.

"Oh fuck me sideways, we are in so much trouble," Selma whispered.

"Yup," Ibis agreed.

"One, Azrael would probably skin anyone alive and keep their skull as a trophy if anyone tried to fuck you sideways," Andrew said in a hushed whisper, "Two, Charlie is fine. He's friendly."

They all groaned, including Oliver.

"My name is Oliver," he huffed from the ledge.

Andrew rolled his eyes and shrugged his shoulders. "I would have stayed with Charlie, but whatever. To each their own."

Ibis tossed her head back and blew the annoying strand of hair that always seemed to make its way into her face at the worse time

"This is ridiculous. I'll go to the Countess myself," Elton seethed as he began his walk to the door.

Selma turned to stop him and paused mid-step as Sooty swooped down quickly with the deadly watering can and smacked him harder on the head than the other times, causing him to fall face first. They all winced and groaned, as if the impact hurt them just as much.

The only one that seemed to enjoy the attack was Oliver, who came down from his ledge and stood behind them, leaning against a column with his legs crossed at the ankles and arms folded over his chest, wearing a smirk.

The Veil clock struck midnight, announcing the lockdown. Elizabeth and Andrew stared at each other and then ran behind the column to get Ronan from hiding. His weakened state worried Elizabeth as he leaned on her to walk. "He needs salt water," she said, as if they should all know this tidbit of information about the merman.

Selma groaned with awareness. "Please tell me this is not Ronan from the book you had me read."

"Um...ok. Sure. It's not Ronan from the book you read," Elizabeth sassed.

Selma stared. Her eyes sliced right through Ibis before they turned to Oliver, then back to Elizabeth and Ronan and then to the ceiling, where the butterflies fluttered around the room. She erupted. With no warning. She lost her shit.

"You didn't," she stated, staring at Elizabeth, who gnawed on her lower lip.

"She didn't," Ibis said. "I did." Might as well admit it. It was just like the saying goes, *in for a penny, in for a pound*. Well, in this case, she was handing her ass on a platinum platter. "I can explain," she started.

"Oh, I'm sure you can. Please, by all means. Explain how you completed a Bring Forth spell?" she asked, beginning to pace, "Without a match? Wait, was that the reason Elton was here?"

"Ew," gagged Elizabeth.

"No. He was here unannounced when I came back earlier."

"Unannounced? That is unacceptable."

"Tell me about it," Ibis agreed.

"Wait. No. We are not changing the subject. One problem at a time."

Ibis pursed her lips and nodded.

"Now tell me what you did. Verbatim."

"I followed the spell as written. I spoke the words clearly and precisely. I used all the correct ingredients and sprinkled the right amount like it..."

"You sprinkled the amount? Sprinkled it where?"

Ibis blinked and then blinked again. Her hands stopped in midair as she mimicked how she sprinkled the items. She looked around and walked to the spot where she recalled the book had fallen. Oliver's eyes followed her, causing a warm invisible blanket to form around her shoulders.

"Around here. The book I was using fell here and well I," she paused, unsure if she should continue to speak since Selma looked like her eyes were going to pop out of her sockets.

"Who told you to sprinkle the powder?"

She licked her lips and swallowed. "N..n..no one. I thought, well, I mean, it just made sense to sprinkle the powder over my book."

Selma covered her eyes with her hands and then ran them through her luscious curls. She nodded towards Seraphina, who swiftly took flight out of the library doors.

"You didn't send for the Countess?" Andrew asked in a high pitch voice.

"Of course not," she fussed back. "Someone grab dipshit from the door and put him somewhere no one else can see him, and don't hit him over the head again," she warned. "How many times has he encountered the watering can?"

Ibis shuffled her feet. "Maybe fou.."

"Twice," Oliver lied. "He will only have an ache in the head."

Chapter Nine
Gargoyles Are Not Cute

He lied for her. She couldn't believe it.

Ibis lowered her gaze. Andrew used his fingers to count and Elizabeth smacked his hands away, but not before Selma caught him. Rolling her eyes and heaving a heavy sigh, she rubbed her temples.

"Where is the spell?"

Ibis chewed on her lower lip. "Upstairs. I'll bring it." Disappointed, she hung her head low and walked to the spiral stairwell. As she was about to step onto the first stair, someone swept her off her feet and held her in powerful arms.

Arms she had become familiar with.

Arms she had laid in.

Read in.

Listened to music.

Even slept in.

Arms that had always made her feel safe and wanted.

Arms that held her tight as he took flight up the center to the higher levels.

In an instant, they landed on her private level. He carried her, surveying her quarters, while she watched him. His profile was strong. Masculine. Everything about him was handsome.

He tucked his wings back and lowered her to the ground, keeping his arm firmly around her waist.

"Little one?" he asked, raising an eyebrow, eyes burning into lavender embers.

"I...um...I think I left the spell by the ledge." She pulled back out of his arms and warmth and shivered. No doubt the blush she sported was as bright as her hair. Searching the area, she found the piece of paper with the cursed spell where Oliver once sat. She waved to Elizabeth below, who gave her two thumbs up and Andrew, who made some odd face before turning to go down the stairwell. She paused and turned, finding Oliver staring at her belongings, including her shelves full of books and fairy lights. One shelf had an open candle. She walked over and stood next to him. He leaned over and sniffed, pulling back. He muttered something she did not understand, and he leaned forward again, sniffing deeper and exhaling.

"It's pine," she said softly.

His zealous eyes turned to her. A soft smile teased his lips and his ears twitched. "Pine," he repeated, as if testing the word. "I like pine." His raspy voice, rumbled in her room. She tucked the spell in her pocket and climbed the built in steps to the top on the opposite end. He pulled her away from the steps and back into his arms, causing them to float above the ground.

"Up there," she pointed, amazed how easily he swept her into his arms and carried her. With one solid flap of his wings, they glided up higher until they reached the large bay windows. He brought her close to the window bench and sat her down. She crawled over the cushion, frowning at his growl. Her fingers unlatched the hook. It was her favorite place to sit and read and just enjoy the outside world. A cool breeze blew in from the opened window, letting in the soft scents of the pine and gardenias behind The Veil.

Oliver peered over her shoulder; his eyes widened in awe. He sniffed the air and closed his eyes, humming to himself.

A squeeze tightened within her chest. She kneeled back on the cushion, taking a deep breath and enjoying the outdoor smells. The crisp air littered her quarters. A Monarch butterfly fluttered around her. Oliver stared at it in wonderment. It landed on one of his horns and made itself at home, opening and closing its wings. Oliver raised his eyes and sat down as to not disturb it.

Ibis giggled, placing a hand over her mouth before she reached up and let the butterfly perch itself on her finger. "These are butterflies," she explained.

"Butterflies," he repeated before snapping at one as it flew close by.

Ibis gasped and swatted them away. "We don't eat butterflies."

"Why?"

"Well, I...we..." she paused and kneeled back on her heels again. "I suppose you could eat them, but it's unnecessary. If you are hungry, I will grab you something from the hearth."

He nodded and leaned his head out the window again, side-eying her before closing his eyes and taking a deep breath. His wings expanded and shivered. A small smile teased his lips.

"Do you want to go outside?"

"Very much."

She chewed her bottom lip and looked around. "Wait here," she whispered before dashing down the small steps.

Soft mutterings from below stopped as soon as she made the center of the library. She handed the spell to Selma. Her annoyed stare combined with Elizabeth's solemn one stopped her in her tracks.

"What now?" she asked.

Elizabeth shrugged her shoulders, leaning into Ronan's embrace. "I told her everything. She knows I gave you the spell and talked you into completing it."

Selma crossed her arms and arched her brow. "All of this to find out if his tail vibrates. Really?"

Someone kill her.

"That is not why I did the spell."

She felt his presence. She should have known he would not wait. He seemed to always be nearby. Part of her loved the idea of him staying close. The other part, like the right now part, was not happy.

"My tail does not convulse. Where does this information come from?"

Everyone pointed to Elizabeth, who shrugged. "It's a theory and a very good one, if you ask me. Plus, the book is freaking hot."

"I have never heard of such creatures," he said.

Andrew snickered. "Guess he has never seen a rattlesnake."

Ibis ignored Andrew as did Oliver. His eyebrow perked up in interest.

"Yeah well, no one thought Gargoyles had curly, cute tails and here you are," Elizabeth sassed back.

He growled. His tail snapping hard against the hardwood floor. "My tail is not cute," he grumbled. "It's a weapon used to disarm, capture and strike. It is lethal, just like the can used to strike the imbecile on the floor."

No.

Not cute.

He was adorable, in a grumpy curly tailed gargoyle sort of way.

"See," Elizabeth said with a wink. "Cute."

Ronan growled

Ibis turned apologetic eyes to Selma. "What did I do wrong with the spell?"

Selma softened her tone. "You were not supposed to sprinkle the powder. You either place the item in the powder or place the powder on the item. Sprinkling the powder unleashes it into the atmosphere. Which means you bring forth items from books read at that moment," she motioned to Ronan and then to the butterflies.

"But Oliver is not from a book," Ibis stated.

As if sensing her distress, Oliver came behind her and sheltered her with his wing. The sudden warmth she felt eased the tension in her body.

"No. He's not," Selma said in a matter-of-fact tone. There was more to the spell. Something Ibis missed. Something Elizabeth missed.

Frick frack, Elizabeth.

"Either way, we need to search The Veil, make sure nothing else has risen from books that we are not aware of. Last thing we need is to alert the Countess of a disastrous event before the Ostara Ball. Or worse. The High Priestess."

Oh no.

It was one thing for the Countess to get involved. But the High Priestess would be worse than setting the library on fire.

"Andrew, I will need you and Ronan to assist me with returning Elton back to his quarters. I will have a memory spell completed. I'm not sure how much it will work, but I will try. After we secure him, you and Elizabeth must go back to your quarters. Take Ronan with you and make sure he does not leave the room. And for Jupiter's sake, clean up the seaweed."

Andrew shoved Elizabeth, only to get shoved back. Ronan watched with humor as Andrew grabbed Elton's leg and began to drag him to the door.

Selma stared at the butterflies and sighed. Ibis watched her friends leave, dragging Elton along the way, muttering something about who's fault everything was before it quieted down. It wasn't long that Seraphina flew back in, chirping and chattering away before turning around and leaving them again.

Selma groaned before turning her gaze to Ibis.

Ibis stood frozen.

"Their quarters is leaking and Azrael is waiting for them."

As if they had heard, Andrew rushed back in with his shoes in hands, followed by Elizabeth and Ronan, who continued to drag Elton. He let him drop on the floor and pushed the door closed.

Andrew pointed to the door and mouthed 'Azrael' as they all scrambled around the room. Selma sashayed to the door as Ibis signaled Elizabeth, Andrew, and Ronan up the spiral staircase. "Just hide upstairs in my quarters!" she yelled.

Selma looked down at Elton, who muttered something and snapped her fingers at Sooty and pointed down at him. Without hesitating, Sooty swooped down with the watering can and smacked Elton over the head again, rendering him unconscious.

Ibis turned to Oliver.

84

For the first time, his arms, not his wings or tails, wrapped around her waist, drawing her in closer. He peered down and tilted his head. Before Ibis could tell him to hide, Selma spoke from behind her.

"Get her out of here," she stated to him.

His eyes flared and without hesitating, he swept her up and flew her to the upper levels, past the second floor, where Elizabeth hid with Ronan. Past the third level where Andrew hid tucked away behind a bookshelf. He swooped through the opening of the still-opened large balcony doors. She squealed as he carried her into the night air.

The stars lit the night sky like distant embers. The cool breeze soothed the inside of his wings and he rejoiced in the feeling. He flew higher into the night, thrilling in the feel of flying. Not just flying, but flying in a world he was unfamiliar with. The lush forest below him beckoned him to come nearer. A tremble in his arms broke through his thoughts.

Ibis.

He drew her closer to his body, cradling her. Lights twinkled from a distance, catching his attention.

"Stay to the left, in the shadows," she pointed to the other side. "That is the town."

Villagers, he thought. He was a Guardian. Meant to protect villagers. Would they not seek him out?

He followed her instructions and cast to the left, remaining in the shadows. Upon descent, he discovered a clearing suitable for landing. He tucked one wing back behind him and the other remained around Ibis, shielding her from the cool breeze. Her tremors slowed.

My Ibis, he thought.

His.

She was so small in his arms. It soothed the beast in him. She curled deeper into his chest, seeking the warmth he provided. His chest swelled, and his arms tightened.

"Still cold, little one?"

Ibis nodded her head and burrowed in deeper. Oliver tucked his wing tighter around her body and scanned the area.

"If you follow the path, there's a greenhouse," she said, peeking her head out from under his wing. Loose tendrils of auburn waves escaped their tie. The wind kicked at her curls, swirling them around into the night. Her dark eyes glowed in the moonlight. He tucked her back into his warmth and followed the path. He stepped lightly, feeling the ground beneath his feet. It was a a mixture of damp softness and cold edges. He did not enjoy either feeling. He grunted as he stepped on something sharp and hissed as he stepped on another.

"Are you alright?"

"The ground is sharp."

She leaned over and pointed ahead. "It's softer on that side," she said. "Grassier."

"Grassier?"

She nodded. "It might be easier if I walked."

He tightened his hold on her. "No. This ground is not safe."

She giggled. "I have walked this path many of times, big guy. I'm sure I will be safe."

A slow rumble started low in his chest, manifesting louder as he continued to carry and hold her close. She placed a hand on his chest.

"You're purring?"

Purring?

"I do not understand this word."

She licked her lips, and his eyes drifted to them, brightening now with interest. She smiled at him.

"It's cute."

He frowned. This was not a word he associated with himself. "Gargoyles are not cute. We are fierce guardians. Lethal and aggressive."

None of this phased her. She leaned into his embrace and sighed. "And cute," she whispered.

Damn purring, whatever this word meant, he thought to himself.

Chapter Ten
Sucking Faces With A Gardenia

Ibis moved around the greenhouse, watering the plants and herbs. Oliver held a small lantern, burning the light low to remain hidden. She hoped Selma would send a sign or a familiar with more information. Now that she thought of it, no one knew where she was and she had no means of contact.

A problem for a later time. Right now, she needed to find something to feed Oliver and a place to rest. Exhaustion made her wary, and she felt chilled to the bone. This time of year, the days were nice and warm, but the nights remained cool.

She gathered a few ingredients from the herb garden. It was a good thing the greenhouse had a backup hearth. Within the cabinets, she found some items she could use to make a quick, simple meal. Even if it was only an herb sandwich. She smashed together the basil and oregano and added cilantro and garlic with a pinch of pepper. After toasting the leftover bread, she spread olive oil inside and then added the herb mixture. She sliced the sandwich into four pieces. Oliver stared at her, unsure, but picked up one section and sniffed it. His eyes glowed curiously before peeking inside the bread. She tried not to smile and took a small bite from her piece.

Sure, it could use bacon, turkey or maybe roasted pork, but she was just hungry and it would have to do. She took another bite and another. Before she realized it, she was done with her piece and he had not taken a bite of his. He handed her his piece.

"Eat, little one."

She shook her head. "There are four slices. Besides, you need to eat. You have had nothing at all."

His frown grew deeper, and he looked at his piece. He took a solid bite and chewed. His brows shot up, surprised, and he took another bite, finishing the section.

"Pretty good, right?" She asked, pleased with herself and with him enjoying the sandwich. It was a mixture her *abuela* had taught her when she was younger. Something quick, easy and filling to eat. There were times Ibis would enjoy the simple sandwich just because it reminded her of her *abuela*.

"I do not understand this meal, but I like it," he said with a soft smile, helping himself to another piece. She wiped her hands and left the third slice for him to enjoy. They argued over who was going to eat the last piece. In the end, Ibis sliced the piece into two parts and they shared it.

"Why is this called a greenhouse? The house does not look green to me," Oliver asked, glancing around the room. "It is a glasshouse."

She giggled. He really was cute, regardless of what he said.

"You're right. It is made of glass. We call it a greenhouse because the glass lets in the sunlight and helps grow the plants inside. These plants," she said, extending her hand out and pointing around, "do not fare well in colder weather. We keep them in here to grow them till it's time to transfer them to the gardens."

She walked him down the aisles explaining each greenery and what its used for. Some were herbs for cooking, others were for healing and other spells. Along the way, they walked down another section of the greenhouse that was recently extended to include flowers and other plant life. As much as Ibis enjoyed the herbs section, she loved the flowers. Gardenias were her favorite. They were in season and blooming, the entire garden smelled with its richly floral scent. Ibis had secured a small pot, and she checked on it. After uprooting the shrub and potting it into a larger planter, she smiled happily to see it growing marvelously.

It was a planter she had worked hard on with its unique paintings. She added her little familiars to the pot along with some of her favorite books.

"This one is mine. I've had it reserved, and she's ready to come home with me," she said, running her fingers over the white petals of the flowers.

Oliver sniffed the plant. His smile widened. "I like this one. Reminds me of you," he whispered the last part.

"Of me?"

"I remember the scent when I awoke. Your quarters."

She smiled. "I have some flowers in the vases around the library."

"It is your home," he stated.

"Yes," she answered. "Do you remember your home?"

He nodded and held his hand out. Without hesitating, she placed her hand in his. He swept her up and walked back over to the fire hearth, where he sat them down and kept her close. One arm draped around her shoulder, keeping her body warm against his. She rested her head on his chest and snuggled up in his embrace.

"I cannot recall much. It's a feeling I have."

"How so?"

"Are there gargoyles here?" he asked.

Her eyes rounded, shaking her head no. The mundanes were aware of The Veil and its inhabitants, but they have never crossed the woods if they did not have a need to. They remained on their side and those that lived at The Veil did the same. Now and then, The Veil ventured into town for supplies. No different when the mundanes came to The Veil for something specific.

"The mind is hazy, in a sense. Part of me wants to tell you I know where I am from, but there is something holding me back. As if I did not exist prior to arriving here. This cannot be, though. How could I not be of this world or any world?"

Her eyes roamed over his face, taking in his wavy shoulder length hair and elongated ears. His violet eyes were enormous and round, flecked and ringed with darker shades of purple. An aquiline nose centered his face, followed by lips both firm and sensual.

She had it bad for him before as a stone gargoyle. Whether from her desk or her loft, she always admired him. Even when she sat many of the times on his lap to read, listen to music or just escape the reality, she felt a certain nearness to him.

"What do you know?"

On their own accord, her fingers ran over his chest. Feeling first the leather encasing his body, the power beneath it. His arm tightened around her.

"I am a gargoyle. I come from a guardian clan. We are a peaceful colony and can co-exist with the mundanes." He paused for a second, frowning and snapping his tail against the floor in agitation.

"Do you have a family?"

"Family?" he whispered.

Did Oliver not know what a family was? Her heart cracked just thinking he was alone in his world.

"We call it family, like a mother or father. Parents. Or anyone else related to you can also be called family. Sometimes, someone not related to you, like friends, can also be considered family."

She thought of her parents, who were long gone, and of her *Tia* and *Abuela*. Then she thought of Elizabeth and Andrew, Selma and Azrael and how she loved them as family. She thought of her familiars and counted them as family as well.

"I cannot recall this," he said again, sadness creeping in with each word. "Birth colony is the same as family. It is where I was born. My parents," he said proudly, as if realizing he was using the word correctly, "should still be at the colony. Gargoyles return to the birth colony to mate."

"Oh," she was not expecting that answer. Something dark and heavy cast over her heart. "Do you have a mate?" she asked, lowering her hand from touching his chest.

His hand reached out and grabbed hers, raising it back up and placing it over his beating heart. Her eyes flew up to his.

"I may not recall many things, but a mate is not something one forgets," he quietly said. "I do not want a mate from my birth colony."

Her breathing stopped. She was sure of it. It was the only thing that would explain this heating sensation in her lungs. This rapid pulsing in her chest. The clamminess in her hands.

She licked her lips, and his eyes followed, glowing brightly.

Oh Goddess.

"I have you, little one," he said, a whisper away from her lips. She hadn't realized how close he moved to her. Or maybe she moved up towards him. Two things were for certain: First, her fingers wrapped themselves in his silky hair. Second, she found herself entranced by his violet eyes before he seized her with a feral kiss, leaving her breathless.

It set her soul on fire.

He ravished her mouth kiss after kiss after kiss, never breaking momentum. Not to adjust her while he helped her straddled his thick thighs. Not when his wings expanded and enveloped her in a warm embrace, shielding her from any additional chill.

Not when she whimpered as his hands caressed down the length of her back and grabbed a handful of her round bottom.

His kiss was hotly tender. They tasted each other deeply. She couldn't help but thrust her fingers through his thick, silky hair and hold on tight. Her thighs clamped around him.

He broke the kiss and muttered something in a growl before returning and reclaiming her lips.

Ditto to whatever he said, she thought.

His hand squeezed her bottom, releasing a soft cry from her lips, and still the kiss went on, unbroken.

A sudden banging of a glass door alerted them of company. They pulled apart and Ibis's eyes rounded. With no notice, Oliver stood up, carrying her and flew up to the ceiling, hiding between the irrigation system and air plants. Ibis remained wrapped around his waist, still straddling him as he held himself perched on the tall trellis.

She remained quiet, waiting to see who was coming in.

"Is she here?" She heard Elizabeth's voice.

A sense of relief washed over her. She placed a soft hand on Oliver's scowling face. His eyes softened to a lavender hue.

She leaned her head against his and wrapped her arms around him before leaning in and dropping a kiss on his lips. His hands tightened on the trellis and he leaned into her more, deepening the kiss before releasing her. They came to the ground, and she unwrapped herself from around him.

Again, the rumbling in his chest began and Ibis did everything in her power to hold back her laugh. She wrapped her arms around his waist since wrapping around his neck while standing was physically impossible for her. Unless he was carrying her. Or she was straddling him.

Oh, she enjoyed that very much.

She leaned her cheek into his chest (on tippy-toes) and sighed. "You're purring again."

"I don't purr," he grumbled, his arms tucking her closer to his body.

She glanced up and smiled. "Yeah, you do, but I won't tell anyone."

He rolled his eyes, something else she found comical about him, before walking around the lower end of the trellis into the greenhouse.

They found Elizabeth and Andrew walking down the aisles. In a hurry, Elizabeth squealed and raced to her, embracing her like she hadn't seen Ibis less than an hour before.

"What happened?"

"What didn't happen?" Andrew said in a huff.

Ibis ignored Elizabeth's constant stare and turned to Andrew. "Just tell me."

"Well, for starters, that Monarch butterfly book you had locked away in your drawer..."

"Yeah?"

"It erupted. Butterflies flew out of the drawer like a swarm. It was chaotic. Sooty is having a field day. It's an open buffet for her, but still. Sheesh."

UGH.

Selma was going to light her hair on fire.

"Elton woke up with not only a headache, but a few knots to go with it and a small memory lapse. He doesn't remember everything. But that has something to do with Rosie. She sat on his head and her eyes went all white. Then he couldn't remember why he was in the library. So all that stuff about Rosie being a rodent, I take it back."

Goddess.

"Oh, Azrael knows."

"Knows what?" Ibis asked, her eyes flashing to Elizabeth, who still stared at her strangely, and then at Andrew.

"Knows everything. You know Selma can't keep secrets from him. They have that whole mind thing."

"Oh no," Ibis muttered. "What did he say?"

"He laughed at the butterfly explosion. Then got pissed with the Elton incident. Then went nuclear when he found out we have two N.O.T.W. at The Veil," he released a loud shrilling whistle.

"N.O.T.W?"

"Not of this world," Andrew clarified. "Don't worry. I asked the same question. Like I'm supposed to know Reaper talk."

"I think it's more Veil Force talk than Reaper talk." Ibis was pretty sure she needed to walk around with a notebook just for The Veil Force and all of their code names.

"Hold on one second," Elizabeth said. Her eyes sliced into small slithers, walking up to Ibis and grabbing her chin, moving it from one side and then the other. Her eyes snapped open.

Wide.

As did her mouth.

"When were you going to tell me?"

Ibis swallowed the guilty knot that formed in her throat.

"Tell you what?"

"Oh, no you don't."

"What did I miss?" asked Andrew.

"Look at her face. She's all flushed. Lips plumped and swollen." Andrew stared at her. A sly smile teased his lips. "Ivy, have you been sucking face?"

She glanced back and caught Oliver's stare from the distance. He stayed behind while she figured out what was happening. Because certain parts of his anatomy needed to be controlled. Sensing her uneasiness, he made his way towards her.

She looked at Andrew and blushed while Elizabeth squealed.

"Oh Goddess. She kissed him," Elizabeth said, twirling in circles.

"Who?" Andrew asked confused, then saw Oliver. "Charlie?" his voice went up a little higher than normal before he coughed and lowered his voice, "You kissed Charlie?"

She loved her friends.

"Well, I wasn't sucking faces with a gardenia."

Chapter Eleven

Quiet Not So Quiet Time

T rust was a fragile thing.

Oliver was not sure if he trusted the witches. Or if he believed the Return-Back spell would reverse the curse all together. There was a possibility the spell could release him and he could return home. Or he could return to stone and remain confined in darkness.

Forever.

Not a prospect he was looking forward to.

So, no.

He did not trust the witches.

However, he did trust Ibis. Her sorrowful eyes tore at him while Selma advised of the consequences it could have. There was something more to the spell Selma could not make out. First, they needed to know where he came from. She requested more time to confirm before completing it.

Now, he waited in her loft, surrounded by her familiars, books and scent.

"Sooty no," he growled, flying after the vexing owl. He swooped up below her. "No, we don't eat butterflies," he warned.

"*Hoooot.*"

"That's not nice," he grumbled, flying back to the loft and setting her on her perch. He placed a sliced apple by her claw and bit into one, showing her how to eat the fruit. He was on his second serving and enjoying every piece. "Try," he encouraged.

She spread her wings wide and opened her beak, bobbing up and down with a screech before kicking the slice down to the ground. He caught it mid-air and sliced his eyes at the miscreant.

"No butterflies," he repeated.

"*Hoooot.*"

"Ibis said no."

A soft giggle from behind him caught his attention. His eyes roamed over Ibis and her curves. She was stunning in a long forest green dress. The long sleeves and bodice ruched together in different shades of green, down to her waist, enticing her figure even more. She held Rosie in her hands while she chomped away at something long and orange. A basket sat in her other hand. Softly, she placed Rosie in the blanket off to the corner.

"Is someone being difficult?"

He remained quiet, blinking once and then again before remembering she asked a question and then growled as Sooty pointed a wing at him.

"Me? You're the one eating butterflies."

"*Hoooot.*"

"No, you cannot." His eyes lit up, annoyed with his new winged friend, before he turned his gaze to Ibis, who was bent over with a hand over her mouth, face red.

"Little one?"

"You are too cute."

Cute.

There was that word again. He straightened to stand full height, towering over her, his wings expanded, making him appear larger. His eyes glowed, stalking her slowly. Her breath came in slow pants. She cautiously stepped back.

Very smart move, but useless.

A flush crept up her chest, neck and onto her beautiful face.

Her back paused at the wall. A wall full of books. Books she favored and read the most, according to her friend Elizabeth. Books Elizabeth suggested he read to get with the times and pop-culture.

Whatever that meant.

"Do you still find me cute, little one? Knowing how small you are compared to me," he placed his wings on the opposite side of her, enclosing her in, yet leaving enough space as to not scare her. "Knowing you are now trapped," his voice was low and smooth. His large hand took her face and cradled it. "Knowing there is no escaping me," brushing his nose against hers.

Soft pants escaped her lips. He inhaled her, practically tasting her scent on his tongue just from breathing her in.

He craved no one like he craved her.

Her touch set his whole being aflame. His wings tingled from the contact. Tenderly, his thumb caressed the apple of her flushed cheek. She leaned deeper into his hand and closed her eyes, smiling.

"Yes," she whispered.

It took him a moment to understand her response and his brows shot up.

"Yes, I do still find you cute," she said, pushing off the wall and moving in closer to him. One hand remained on his chest while the other came up into his hair. He bent lower, letting her run her fingers through his mane. "Especially when you purr."

He moved his hand further into the long auburn tresses of her hair and with his free hand, lifted her up by the waist. She wrapped her legs around him, and he held her close.

Her lips parted with a soft gasp, her face now near his. Eyelashes fluttered against his cheek. The purring she referred to grew deeper.

Time seemed to pause. Maybe it was her eyes. Maybe it was her smile or that soft gasp as she grounded her hips against his.

Whatever there was, he knew at that exact moment he did not want the Return-Back spell to work.

The curses be damned.

The witches that cursed him in the first place be damned.

He wanted Ibis.

The word kept repeating itself over and repeatedly.

There was no reasoning with it.

No stopping it.

No fighting it.

She was his.

His *little one.*

His mate.

Fire.

Completely and utterly on fire.

There was no other explanation for this burning sensation engulf-ing her. The urgent need.

The raw desire.

It was maddening and intoxicating.

His long fingers threaded through her wild hair, gripping tightly, while the other hand held her securely. A moan escaped her lips as she ground her hips against him. Hands squeezed her tighter and lips met in a wild, earth-shattering kiss. Neither seemed to want to end, and still they continued to take and give. She captured his lips, kissing, suckling, nibbling, drawing out a growl from him. He returned the favor with a possessive kiss.

Greedy for more.

Breathless, she pulled back.

Time paused.

Like a movie she saw once, where the girl leans back and stares into the eyes of her star-cross lover with blind desire. He returns the stare boldly, eyes fully dilated and filled with heat.

She squirmed against him. Frantic hands gripping him tightly. His hand encouraged her hips to move.

Goddess.

She was acting shameful, and she didn't care one damn bit. Her *Tia* would surely cast her out if this got out.

A devilish smile teased her lips.

"Little one," he whispered.

No talking.

She didn't want to talk.

She wanted him.

Only him.

All of him.

"Someone is coming," he growled, pulling away. His ears twitched at the sounds echoing louder from below.

She groaned. "Ugh, someone is always coming," she muttered into his chest, "Except me," disentangling her legs from his waist, releasing him.

Oliver's eyes glowed and nostrils flared. An extremely heated intensity jutted out from his aura.

His eyes did something to her.

Something deep inside.

It made her quiver.

Made her yearn.

Made her want to explore the depths of purple hues.

The library doors squeaked open, allowing intruding voices to filter in. Voices known as The Order. They came in every evening, putting away their scrolls and other borrowed items. On rare occasions, someone would take out the Golden Key from the library and then return it. It was the only time Ibis needed to be present, since she held the Onyx Key to lock the enchanting casing.

We can thank the Goddess that such a task was not required.

Ibis took a deep breath, remaining close to Oliver, who continued to stare hungrily at her. Shadows and darkness enveloped the halls as the timer in the library dimmed the lights. Hoping this would prevent those who walked in late to notice the missing statue from the center.

Silently, Ibis walked by the loft, staying hidden within the shadows, and watched The Order place the scrolls and artifacts into the cart for her to catalog in the morning. Warmth spread around her back and a sudden wisp of air flittered near her neck. Leathery wings encased her against the banister, hiding her even more in the shadows, while Oliver stood close behind her.

So close.

Close enough to lean forward and inhale her scent.

Close enough for his lips to brush the side of her neck, scraping his teeth over her skin.

Close enough for her entire body to tingle at his touch.

Hands traced the contours of her figure. He ran a fingernail up her side and then back down, drawing a shiver out of her with each passing.

Her breath hitched.

"Do you think you can remain quiet?" Humor laced his voice.

She turned her face up and lifted herself on her toes to reach his lips. He met her halfway, deepening the kiss.

"Can you?" she whispered back.

Emotions catapulted.

From existing in a dreamlike state to a cold splash of reality only to slowly succumbed to the aching desires within her. His lips moved down her throat while his hands came around her, holding her close. Spreading across her lower stomach. She never felt insecure about her body, but for once, Ibis was unsure of her belly. She was curvy in every sense. Had been since she was a child. She loved her curves. Celebrated them. Why she felt the need to stop his hands was beyond her.

His low warning hiss stopped her from preventing his touch. She turned her face and his lips brushed over hers. She released his hands and leaned back into his body. The look in his eyes, the fire and need, matched her own desires. One hand remained low on her belly, gently squeezing her softness and releasing a deep groan against her ear, while the other trailed a heated path down her thigh. She bit her lower lip, stopping the whimper from escaping.

She was losing the battle of remaining quiet. There was no way. How could she when his lips heated her skin and his hands kneaded and squeezed every inch of her? Flustered and achy, she rotated her hips, letting her hands slide down his thighs and holding on tightly. Mindlessly grinding against him. Her stomach muscles quivered as his hand moved lower and lower. The one on her thigh pulled her dress higher and higher, till his hands touched her bare skin.

Heat radiated from his palm as if he was branding her. So hot and smooth against her skin. She sighed just from the feel of them.

"Hush, little one. We still have company."

Easier said than done. She was on fire and about to jump out of her own freaking skin. His touch was addictive. Never had she felt this way before. No one had set her on fire like Oliver.

He ran his fingers along the edge of her panties.

"Your scent is driving me mad." His lips grazed her outer ear.

Mad.

Insane.

Crazed.

Yes. She was feeling all of that and then some.

"Show me how you like to be touched."

She bit her lower lip. No one had ever asked her to do that. She broke eye contact and lowered her head. The hand kneading her belly left its position and boldly slid up her abdomen over her chest and raised her chin to meet his eyes.

The deep rumbling in his chest grew louder. His nose brushed against hers and lips teased the corner of her mouth. "Show me, my little Ibis."

Something bold grew inside her.

Encouraging her.

Without breaking eye contact, she lowered her hand and covered his, the one continuing to tease the lacy edges of her underwear. Lust consumed her, using both his hand and hers to stroke and pet herself. His mouth devoured hers, capturing every moan, every sigh, every plea. She writhed against his hand, lost in the pleasure.

Ibis didn't hesitate. She twisted in his embrace, colliding with the railing and nearly toppling over a blasted statue in the corner. Whispering from below alerted them to hearing the noises.

She didn't care. Need pulsed in her veins and from the intense glow of Oliver's eyes, neither did he. Strong arms hoisted her up against him. Her legs wrapped around his waist eagerly. He backed away from the railing, slowly letting the shadows consume them more till his back collided with one of her bookshelves. It rattled slightly, and she placed a hand on the stupid ledge to steady it.

She held on tight.

Thrills ran up and down her body.

"More. Give me more," he demanded.

She ground her hips recklessly into his palm as he curved his fingers to stroke her deeper.

Relentlessly.

"Oliver." A breathy little moan escaped her lips.

He worked her into a frenzy, building the tension inside her till her body clenched. Frantic hands gripped his shoulders. Pleasure shot through her, exploding in quivering waves.

Chapter Twelve
Distractions and Methods

S oft morning light squeaked in between the closed drapes. A small sliver of light peered in and land directly on Ibis's face. Her hands came up to block the dreaded ray. A rustling sound made her open her eyes.

"Hooot."

She glared at Sooty, flying around the ceiling, chasing after butterflies and enjoying her morning feast. Chaos laid contently at the edge of the bed, purring and bathing her paws while Rosie and Kit snuggled close on the small pillow in the corner. Every other breath, Rosie's foot would thump and Kit's tail twitched. No doubt dreaming.

Warmth surrounded her, along with a strong heavy arm around her waist. She smiled, thinking of all the ways Oliver learned to touch her and she him in return. They nestled together in a tangled web of arms and legs. He tucked his wings behind him and settled for the blanket she pulled over them. This was something he was unsure. Never had he seen a blanket before but once she pulled it over them and he the soft texture of the blanket, he purred and burrowed deeper into the blanket, snuggling her closer.

She made a mental note to find a larger blanket.

Cozier.

Softer.

There were several things she needed to get accomplished. First, she needed to make sure something properly clad Oliver. He wore whatever armor he had after being released from the curse. When they settled in for the night, she helped him take it off. With a wince, he rubbed his shoulders and stretched his arms and wings, groaning from being strapped in the leather bindings for so long. His pants showed signs of wear and tear. Where on Jupiter's moon was she going to find pants to fit him was beyond her, but she would figure it out? Maybe Selma could spell an outfit for him or the High Guards might have something for him to wear. It wasn't as if they had seven-foot witches walking around the perimeter.

The next thing they needed was a story for him. A lie. A small fib. Nothing too serious. Maybe nobody would notice the enormous giant Gargoyle statue missing from the library. After all, it wasn't as if witches walked in and took selfies with him.

Maybe that should be the first thing she worked on and then find his clothes. Either way, both needed to be rectified this morning.

She sighed.

The sun light gleamed brighter through the opening.

Forget it.

Both items are a later problem.

She snuggled deeper into his embrace, enjoying how he tightened his arm around her waist and pulled her even closer. A lusty feeling of warmth washed over her.

Shameful, she thought to herself. But oh, how she loved it.

She lifted the secured blanket from her side and turned in his arms, snaking her arm around his waist. Her smile faltered and body froze.

It couldn't be.

Who was this man in her bed?

Man?

It's a man! In her bed!

A man with wings?

She pulled her arm from around his waist and sat up on the bed, snatching the blankets up and covering herself. Not that she needed to. She was not naked, although she might as well have been with the slip she wore to bed. She changed into it last night to drive Oliver mad with lust.

Which it worked.

Several times.

Crawling backwards, she crept closer to the edge of the bed, swinging her foot to make sure she touched the floor. She studied the mysterious man, with high cheekbones and a sharp nose. Strong jawline and messy dark hair covered his pointy ears. Skin tanned as if he had just come in from a day on the beach. Soft wings laid flat against his back, resting.

She leaned one knee on the bed, easing closer to get a better look. She pulled the covers down, revealing his bare chest and abdomen any male would be jealous of.

He stirred and rolled over. His arm reached out over her side. Broad shoulders with smooth, leathery wings. Etched in his skin was the marking she carved, *I.M.H.* surrounded by a heart.

Goddess.

Oliver was human!

Well, sort of in another worldly kind of way. She found him attractive in his gargoyle form but here, now, lying in her bed, with her beating heart drumming out of control, he entranced her.

She gasped and pulled back, not realizing her footing was not all the way on the floor. She fell backwards off the bed, landing right on her rear.

Jupiter's balls that hurt.

She winced, moving from the floor. Ignoring Chaos's meows, she got on her knees and peeked over the mattress, hoping Oliver did not witness her ungraceful landing.

If she thought it complicated before things with a missing gargoyle now awoken and roaming the library, she didn't think things through. How was she going to explain the mighty tall, mighty gorgeous, mighty Elf-like stranger hanging out in the library? Technically, she could fabricate a story of Oliver being a visitor from another Order, paying a visit for the Ostara Ball. It wouldn't be uncommon or unheard of.

Oh, who was she kidding? Everyone was going to notice Oliver. There was no hiding him. Plus, The Veil was like a magnet for the gossip mongrels. It was hard to keep secrets here. The only reason no one had discovered him, or her for that matter, was because she kept to herself and went unnoticed.

For the most part.

At least she hoped she went unnoticed.

Focus Ibis. No time to go down a rabbit hole.

She peeked over the mattress, eyes colliding with a pair of bright lavender ones. Hers rounded before she squealed as muscular arms reached out and hauled her back onto the bed, over the covers and under a very warm, very hard, breathing body.

Oliver's lips trailed down her neck, releasing a groan.

"You smell divine, little one."

Distractions.

A definite distraction. Oh, but she loved this distraction.

She needed to focus. Focus on what? How was she going to focus when his lips were driving her mad? A shiver raced down her spine like lightning.

Lightning? No, that was not what she needed to focus on. Oliver. The man version of Oliver. Yes. That was what she needed to focus on.

"You can shift?" she panted in between each kiss and nibble he gave on her skin.

He grumbled something incoherent before slightly raising and staring down at her. "I do not know this word." Oliver tilted his head curiously at her. She snagged her bottom lip and stroked her finger over his cheek.

"You shift forms. You're you, but not really you," she fumbled with her words. "I mean, you do not look the same."

His eyes soften, and he leaned into her hand. "I am the same only in daylight. I do not shift, as you call it."

"So gargoyles don't turn to stone to sleep?"

Oliver chuckled. "First a convulsing tail and now stone sleeping? What other ludicrous ideas are there of my kind in your beautiful mind, little one?"

She giggled. "Honestly, I am not sure I want to share them with you now."

111

"But you must. How else am I to dispel the illogical logics of The Veil?" His eyes grew openly amused.

Her lips trembled with the need to smile. "I am a witch. All of my illogical logics can be dispelled simply with a book."

He leaned forward. Nose to nose. Lips gently brushing hers as he spoke, "Hmmm, that may be true my little Ibis, but where is the fun in that when you have an illogical being in question within your grasp, willing to answer anything you ask." His lips traced a heated path down her neck. Her heart pounded erratically. "Do anything you desire," he whispered huskily.

Goddess.

There was no focusing at this point. She shifted in his arms, pulling back to bring him face to face. Her heated stare locked on his and she kissed him.

Not just any kiss.

Oh no, Ibis Heliodoro, Light Witch of The Order, ravished her gargoyle lover. In return, Oliver's demanding lips parted hers, deepening the kiss. The kiss alone sent fresh waves of euphoria. With every touch of his lips, slide of his tongue, brush of his hands, grind of his hips, Ibis's pleasure radiated.

His hands slid across her side, squeezing her hip. "I cannot resist you, my little Ibis."

A sultry smile teased her lips. "Then don't."

A powerful force passed between them, a maddening desire threatening to set them both ablaze. He drove her wild with distraction. She drove him insane with lust. She carelessly tossed her slip of a dress somewhere and laid it on the ground, while he dragged off his frayed pants and scrunched them at the end of the bed in no time.

Skin to skin, heat to heat, they touched, caressed, explored each other. He parted her thighs, teasing her. Rubbing without entering. She couldn't take it anymore. She rotated her hips in slow circles, teasing him in return. Relishing the low growl, he released. His large hands gripped her hips, raising her slightly off the bed. She felt him at the tip of her entrance.

His eyes searched hers as if asking for permission.

She reached up, brushing her lips over his, silently communicating her approval. Slowly, he slid inside her. She rotated her hips in slow circles, his girth stretching her with each thrust.

Goddess, she was full. So full it hurt in the sweetest way.

"You're mine, little Ibis," he moaned deeply into her ear. Clasping her hips, pulling her into each thrust.

She stretched and melted around his length, feeling every nerve in her body give in to the molten heat exploding within her.

"Oliver," she gasped. Her hips rose to meet him, arching her back. He swallowed her plea, sinking even deeper, stretching her to the limit, and still she ached for more.

Demanded more.

Needed more.

She gave into the moment with total surrender. Her senses shattered. Her body clenched around him as an explosion of pleasure ripped through her, robbing her of her senses.

He stiffened and convulsed, a roar of satisfaction erupted from his lips, eyes glowing brightly before he came down and rested his forehead against hers.

Sharing the same breath.

Hearts beating the same rhythm.

"You're mine, little Ibis."

She closed her eyes, a small smile teasing her lips.

"Yours," she whispered back.

Oliver couldn't take his eyes off of Ibis.

My little Ibis.

As he observed her tidying up their loft, gathering their clothes and arranging items that had been knocked off the shelves during their intimate encounter, the sound of his chest rumbling became louder. A satisfied warmth grew in his belly, as did pride.

His Ibis was an amazing female. Loyal and kind. Beautiful and sexy. Smart and sassy. Bewitching. Most of all, she was thoughtful and caring.

He blinked lazily, staring up at the ceiling at the butterflies swirling around. Now and then, Sooty would swoop by and capture one.

Wretched bird.

A sudden attack of cloth landed on his face. He sat up quickly, glancing around, and spotted Ibis giggling in the corner.

"Sorry," she sheepishly said.

Oh, his little Ibis was not sorry. Not sorry at all.

He tossed the cloth to the floor and prepared his attack.

"No. Don't you dare," she warned, half laughing, half serious. "I need to shower, and I can't have any more distractions," she said.

He tilted his head. "What's a little harm in the form of distractions?" His wings expanded, and he flew to her faster than she expected. She squealed, caught in his arms.

"Shower?" he asked curiously. "Does this mean it's raining outside?"

"No big guy." She drew her arms tighter around his neck. He held her up, not letting her feet touch the ground. "It's like a bath but standing up."

His eyes lit up.

Shower, he thought to himself.

"I like this idea." He shifted her in his arms, cradling her. Uncaring that it completely exposed him in her loft. "Where is this shower?" he asked, enjoying her laugh. She pointed to a door off to the side.

"Will this shower hold the both of us?"

She tightened her hold on him.

"Let's find out."

Chapter Thirteen
An Uncertain Decision

L aundry and cleaning were one of Ibis's favorite days. To some, it was pure torture. But to Ibis, the mundane work of washing clothes and freshening up her little living quarters was special to her. She loved opening the balcony doors and letting in the fresh smell of gardenias from outside. Along with the warmth of sunlight and cool breeze.

Most of all, she loved updating her bookshelves with her current reads and her books pending to be read. Some books she recently pulled were on gargoyles. Oliver found it amusing and somewhat interesting how many lores there were on his kind.

After their discovery of methods on how to use the shower together and running out of hot water along the process, they dried off and dressed. She cleaned up the library's floor and dusted the tables on the various floors. Oliver assisted with lifting the furniture and getting to the areas she would never reach.

It was during their cleaning extravaganza that Oliver offered some answers to her earlier questions. She was delighted to learn gargoyles do stone-sleep, but only when they are in a weakened state. They in fact do not have vibrating tails and although she argued with him, he was a shifter, he stated he was not. He was the same and not shifting into anything.

Ibis rolled her eyes and added stubborn to a gargoyle's quality. It was then she remembered Oliver did not believe vibrating tails existed. She sent him with Sooty and Chaos to research rattlesnakes. He chuckled at the ridiculous name. Wait until he finds out they are venomous.

Ibis was changing the sheets on her bed and adding a new cozy blanket when she heard the library doors squeak open.

Jupiter hairy balls.

She did not expect to find *Tia Isa* standing in her loft, casually looking through her books and other items on her shelf. She swallowed the sudden knot forming in the back of her throat. Chaos jumped on the blanket covering Oliver's armor, laying comfortably as if she belonged there while Kit snuggled near the edge, chewing on some random stick only Goddess knew where she found it.

She cleared her throat and stepped out, closing the door behind her. She folded her hands in front of her and waited.

"Buenos dias."

Ibis smiled stiffly before greeting in return. *"Buenos dias, Tia."*

"I cannot remember the last time I was up here. It has been so long," she said in a quiet voice. Her finger brushing against the bookshelf and then wiping it off against her suit jacket.

As long as Ibis could remember, her *Tia* always dressed in luscious, tailored suits in gorgeous patterns and vibrant colors. Regardless of *Tia* Isa's ancient views, she was modern. Dress-code was one of them. Her *Tia* believed women should be able to express themselves freely. It was one reason The Veil did not follow the uniform code that many other Covens did. It was common for dress-codes to be enforced. The Briar required their colors to be worn. Others had similar requirements. The Veil broke this tradition at the turn of the twentieth century.

If only *Tia* would allow for witches to mate who they preferred and not who they were better matched with because of magic.

"How are you doing?" Ibis asked, walking over to the bed, picking up her scattered dress and underwear from the evening before. She hoped her cheeks did not flare up and if they did, she really hoped her *Tia* did not notice or did not question it.

Her aunt shrugged her shoulder. Such an unusual answer from her. "I have been better. I..." she stopped and sighed, "We have guests arriving from The Briar. I thought it best for you to return to the quarters and offer the loft as a guest room."

She froze.

The loft was her place. Her quarters.

The familiars lived in the library. It was their home. She would not move them. Her eyes shifted to the space where Oliver sat stoned. She couldn't leave Oliver either.

She stood straight, prepared for the backlash. "I don't think me returning to the main quarters is a good idea," she responded. She braced. Waiting.

A few minutes passed before her *Tia* spoke. "*Está bien,*" she said with another shrug, rubbing her two fingers together before turning to the stairwell.

"Wait. That's it?" She came all this way for that?

Her plucked eyebrow arched over dark brown eyes. Eyes darker than hers. Eyes every Heliodoro had. "*¿Qué más quieres?*"

Ibis stared. "I don't understand why you would come here to tell me it would be better to return to the main quarters only to shrug and move on when I tell you I am not going to."

She crossed her arms. Her dark blue suit jacket tugged and crinkled over her arms as she leaned over. "If I demand for you to move to the main quarters, are you going to do it?" Her head tilted to the side, arching a challenging eyebrow.

"No," Ibis responded back, tossing her arms in the air.

"*¡Ya ves! Entonces, ¿en qué quedamos?* You wish to stay here. Then stay here."

"That cannot be the reason you came to see me."

"Why not?"

"Because it is a trivial matter. You would have sent Azrael or Selma. Even Mona, of all people, to ask me. But never you."

"*¡Ay Ibis! No puedo con las estupideces.*"

"It's not stupid. Why *Tia?*"

Tia Isa glared at her. Maybe it was wrong to question her. To push her for an answer. But dammit, she deserved one.

With just a stare, *Tia Isa* froze her over. "You will address me as countess," her voice lowered.

As if struck, Ibis flinched and nodded. Her face flushed with anger. From behind her *Tia*, Oliver glided and crouched low. His eyes glowed with anger. She tilted her head, hoping he would understand and remain hidden less there would be more damage and hell to pay.

"I will not tolerate insubordination from anyone, especially from you. Remember that," *Tia Isa* hissed, grabbing the bottom of her suit jacket and tugging it down before she turned on her heels and marched down the spiral stairwell.

Ibis followed her and stood at the top, watching her leave, but not before *Tia Isa* turned and stared back. Sadness and something more crept into her eyes before she blinked them away and closed the door behind her.

Ibis's shoulder sagged. She sensed Oliver before she felt his hand. Turning, she buried her face in his chest, wrapping her arms around him, inhaling his scent. Soothing her nerves and calming the shit-storm brewing in her heart.

He pulled her back, raising her face up to meet his eyes. Eyes that held fire and anger on her behalf. But there was something else there.

Something more.

"Oliver?"

"The witch you spoke with," he growled menacingly.

Ibis looked away. Her voice wavered. "My *Tia Isa*."

"*Tia Isa*?"

"She is my aunt."

"Aunt? Explain this word." He gritted his teeth.

"She is family," she said in a hushed whisper.

He released her, stepping away from her, setting off silent alarm bells in her mind.

"Family," he spat.

No.

His Ibis was not like them. Not like the witches that cursed him.

But they were family. Family was important. Family meant something to them. Ibis explained this to him.

The nagging voices in his head told him to stop. Another part warned him not to listen to her.

To be wary.

Tread lightly.

How could he trust her when it was her family who summoned him and then cursed him?

"Oliver?"

Her voice. He muttered a curse, knowing she would not understand his language, and turned away from her, avoiding her soft tone and concerned eyes. The silence that followed suffocated him. It smothered the room.

"Oh Goddess," she whimpered.

He closed his eyes, bowing his eyes.

"It was her. My...she...*Tia Isa* did this to you."

The ache in her voice was his undoing. Filled with pain and betrayal. Both feelings he was aware of and trying his hardest not to let it consume him.

Damn curses..

Damn witches.

As Andrew would say, this sucks Jupiter's hairy balls. Not that he understood what any of that meant. He was not sure who Jupiter was and why anyone would want to suck his hairy balls.

It was a strange world.

Bizarre.

Still, it was the only one he was aware of. Try as he might, he could not conjure up his memories or thoughts. It was infuriating not knowing his past almost as much as having to face the idea of going back to it blindly. It was as if he would be returning to darkness.

"I need to go to her," she muttered. "Maybe I can ask her and find out where you came from."

He tilted his head and arched an eyebrow. "She does not appear to be someone who will discuss anything."

"Yes, but, maybe if I...if I agree to return to the main quarters for the Ostara Ball, she might be more inclined to answer some questions for me."

From above, Rosie thumped her foot multiple times while Chaos whined. Sooty rolled her neck, blinking just as Kit crouched low, placing her furry face on her front paws.

Uncertainty crept into her expression. She chewed on her lower lip and glanced away, rubbing her hands together. Her anguish burned a hole in his chest, cooling the angry flames inside.

Gently, he reached his hand out and brushed his thumb off her lip. "I will not let you give up your home."

"But I wouldn't be. It would only be for Ostara."

"Hooot," Sooty disagreed.

"Oh, go chase a butterfly," Ibis snapped.

"Sooty, no. Butterflies are our friends. No chasing," he corrected in a soothing voice. Her feathers ruffled, and she rolled her big brown eyes at him.

Ibis lifted her chin and placed her hands on her hips. A stance of defiance. She boldly met his eyes. He bit the inside of his cheek to keep from smiling.

"I'm going to change and then head to the main quarters," she responded, walking past him to collect her clothes.

He gritted his teeth.

Defiant indeed.

"I don't know this, Ostara. They can find somewhere else to stay. This is your home."

He clenched his mouth tighter.

She turned from an opening on the wall containing her clothes. He frowned at the secret passageway and peeked at it curiously. One hand fell on his arm.

"It's a closet," she said, with a hint of humor in her tone.

"Where does it lead?"

She chuckled, "No where. See? It just holds my stuff." She moved the clothes around the secret room, explaining the drawers and shoe rack.

Indeed, a strange world.

He placed his hand over hers and pulled her near. "Little one," he whispered. "Don't give ..."

"I have to do this," she leaned in and whispered back. "It's the only way we are going to get answers for you."

After grabbing her dress and shoes, she changed rapidly. For a moment, he studied her and then drank up every dip and curve as she changed into an orange dress that hugged her. She added a black leather belt, cinching her waist. He was tongue tied between the low bodice cut, accentuated curves, and her long waves brushed down her back.

His little Ibis.

"And what if I do not care to find out those answers?"

The rumbling in his chest began, and he caught himself, but not before she heard him and turned, midway with the brush in her hair.

Her brown eyes lit with a golden glow. Her face flushed as she ran the brush once more through her hair.

"You don't mean that."

He shrugged his shoulder.

"Oliver, they summoned you here for a reason. I don't know for what or why, but we need to find out. If there is a way to reverse the spell and give you back your freedom, then I am going to do that."

Her fingers fluttered to her neck and heat flushed her apple cheeks.

"And again, little one, at what cost? To become stone again? To return to where ever I was brought forth from?"

To losing you?

"I won't let them turn you to stone again," her voice broke.

His breath caught. A heaviness centered in his chest. Without needing any words, he reached out and wrapped her in his embrace, swallowing the soft gasp that escaped her lips.

Fuck it.

He would deal with the damn witches and damn curses later. This second, he needed her. Her taste drove him mad. Her scent consumed him. Her curves were his to caress. His hands closed over her hips. "My little Ibis, I would rather stay here and be stone for another century listening to your voice in darkness than to be sent back to another world where I could never hear you again."

For the first time since awakening, the uncertainty was daunting.

Chapter Fourteen

A Luz Dragon

She shouldn't be doing this. But what choice did she have?

Oliver needed answers.

She needed answers, and *Tia Isa* had them.

With a heavy heart, she left Oliver wandering the library. She located a section on gargoyles and had him looking through the entire catalog along with other lores. Curiosity drew him in as he flipped through the page after page. Most of it he could not read, but that did not stop him from scrolling through all the pictures. Sooty sat and translated the text for him. It warmed her heart, capturing Oliver and his larger-than-life self, sitting snug between the bookshelves on the floor with Sooty perched on his shoulder, pointing with her feathers at pictures and hooting away. She even brought him glasses to wear. Not that he needed them. Kit snickered when Oliver put them on and curled next to his lap while Rosie and Chaos snuggled on his lap and snoozed away.

Her heart melted. Warmth spread through her belly at the sight of them.

He scoffed at the theories documented on gargoyles, finding it comical. Others he nodded and remained quiet. Determined and mind made up, she left them to their reading.

The main living quarters were across the duo quarters, almost on the opposite side. It was quiet during midday. Most times, everyone strolled the grounds and took advantage of the warmer weather. Especially with the Ostara Ball. Everyone was out preparing for the event. If they weren't in town shopping, then they would be outside in the gardens, organizing and setting up.

With Spring's arrival, Casting Cove was a little hidden oasis. The town loved their privacy and they did not mind keeping their hidden gem to themselves.

Coming to the end of the grand hall, Ibis turned down Sentinel Hall. This led to The Veil Force quarters. Or what they all call the V.F. room. She crossed her fingers and hoped she could locate clothing for Oliver and walk away without questions or curious stares. It's not every day a librarian walked into the V.F. room and asked for clothes to dress a seven-foot gargoyle.

The double doors to the V.F. were ajar. The room was half lit. Squeaky, eerie sounds echoed inside. On the table, she located an illuminescent lantern. With a snap of her fingers, a gold spark flickered the lantern to life. Ibis raised the lantern and peered into the vast darkness. Her skin prickled and her breath came in short pants. Someone or something was near. She could feel their presence.

A warm breath blew across her shoulders from her left.

"Don't move," came the deep voice.

A tsunami of apprehension swept through her. Her eyes collided with Azrael. His hooded cloak hung behind him, revealing his skeletal face and red eyes. Her eyes darted around and snapped shut as another huff of hot air blew her hair off her shoulders. She tried. Goddess, she tried not to flinch. Not to move. Panic like she's never felt before welled in her throat.

"Ibis, look at me," Azrael said calmly.

Icy fear twisted inside her. Deep breath in and out. She opened her eyes.

"Blow the light out," his voice remained low and calm.

"What?" she whispered.

"It's a *Luz* dragon. It's attracted to the light."

Dragon?

Dragon!

They had a frick frack dragon at The Veil?

Oh, Jupiter's hairy balls. She was in trouble.

"Please tell me it's not because of the spell," she whispered.

Even though Azrael was not in human form, she could still imagine him arching his dark eyebrow at her.

"We will discuss that after you snuff out the light," he still said in a low voice, but not as calm as he was before.

"I can't see in the dark." Panic rioted within her.

"I can," Azrael assured her.

"So can I, little one."

Oliver!

She turned in an instant.

Heart stopping at the sound of his voice. A gush of hot air blew at her face, causing her to look up. She turned and faced the heat, coming face to face with a large snout. Opal eyes blinked at her right, sniffing her hair. Its split tongue came out and licked its lips, leaving droplets of drool on the floor at her feet. She flinched, backing away. A mistake, she realized too late. Before she even realized what was happening, the

Luz dragon pulled back its lips, showing large ridged teeth. It opened its mouth, inhaling a gulp of air.

"Ibis!" Azrael yelled.

She blinked.

Time paused.

One minute she stood in front of the Dragon's mouth about to be inhaled and the next Oliver swooped in, folding her in his arms and wings, protecting her tightly inside his stone-like body while Azrael blocked the blazing fire released from the dragon's mouth with his shield around them.

Then time continued.

She clenched her arms around Oliver's neck in a fierce hold. She breathed in shallow, quick gasps and pulled back.

His hands held her close, eyes piercing hers, waiting for her to speak.

"You protected me."

"Always, my little Ibis. Never doubt that."

Oliver slammed the book.

It couldn't be. He paced back and forth down the aisle. Sooty lowered her head within her feathers while Kit and Chaos sat behind the pillars. Rosie hopped closer to him. Thumping her leg once. Then again, harder to grab his attention. She stood on her hind legs and he picked her up, cradling her in one arm.

"It does not matter what the book states," he muttered. Rosie's teeth clicked together multiple times before laying her head against his chest.

"Hooot," Sooty said.

Damn witches.

Damn curses.

"No," he whispered, nuzzling her head. "Do not apologize. You are not to blame."

Of all the fucking places he thought he was from, he didn't expect it to be from a *Myth and Folklore* tome. No wonder he did not remember his past. It was because he didn't fucking have one.

Could the world be this cruel?

He believed himself to be a guardian. It made no sense why he felt this way or knew the things he knew about himself and yet he knew fucking nothing at the same time.

To think they came upon the book by chance. A book sitting in Ibis's cart to return to the locked chambers, as Sooty advised. Only Ibis had the key to complete this. It was a mystery why they left the book out in the open.

But then again?

He glared at the book, picking it up with a snarl. The smell was familiar. Almost too familiar. The same smells from when he first arrived. A distinct smell he recognized earlier.

Family *Tia Isa's* fragrance was all over the book. His upper lip rose and nostrils widen. She would continue to be a bane in his existence.

Frick frack curses.

Frick frack witches.

He caught himself, stopping short and standing tall. Now he sounded like Ibis.

Ibis.

His little Ibis.

Just the sound of her name drifting into his mind brought an inner peace to his soul. The anger he felt faded away, turning to dejection. If the return spell worked, he would go back to the book.

A life of non-existence.

A life without Ibis.

Unfortunately, this world was cruel.

"Hooot."

He glanced around the quarters he had inhabited. Whether by choice, this was the closest thing to a proper home he ever had.

"I will see if there is a way to manipulate the spell." Thinking over Sooty's plan of changing the spell. The wise owl stated spells could be altered as long as they were specific. If they specified who was to be returned, then maybe, just maybe, he had a chance of staying and not returning to that blasted myth tome he was from.

He closed his eyes, feeling out the library in search of Ibis. Last he remembered she was going upstairs. Unsure if the spiral staircase would hold him, he released his wings and flew up the levels, hovering over the rails. She was not in the room. Only a recent lingering scent of her. His ears perked as stumbling footsteps from the hallway trampled closer. Gliding down, he tucked his wings back as far as he could hide them and stalked down the aisles down into the center towards the double doors. Andrew and Elizabeth held his eyes with a frantic stare. Unease slithered down his spine as they requested for Ibis. His ears twitched at a distant rumbling from beyond the doors. A faint smog odor drifted in.

Sooty screeched and flapped her wings wildly, and Kit and Chaos hissed. Rosie clicked her teeth viciously and thumped her foot.

Ibis!

Without hesitating, he flew down the hall, catching her scent behind another pair of large doors. He sensed the reptilian beast.

Winded and alert, Elizabeth and Andrew arrived. Both were apprehensive that something may go wrong.

"It's a *Luz* dragon," Andrew whispered.

"It escaped the book held by a Veil Force," Elizabeth said.

They stayed close behind him, looking over from behind his wings into the darkness. His eyes focused into the shadows. The sooty smell intensified.

Suddenly, his little Ibis's fear slammed into him. She stood still while the beast stalked her from her side. Breathing over her. Scenting her with his redolent.

Another male was inside with her. Darkness recognized darkness and yet he sensed no immediate threat from him.

It wasn't till Ibis's initial shock of hearing his voice did the reptilian beast react with the light and threaten her.

Oliver didn't think.

Didn't hesitate.

Time stopped as he raced to her, enclosing her in his arms. Encasing them both in his wings. Energy surged from behind him. Elizabeth and Andrew joined hands and slowed time, enough to affect the *Luz* dragon's mobility. Enough to allow Oliver the ability to reach Ibis and protect her. Enough time for the other male to come over and shield them both from the dragon's blazes. Oliver snuffed the light out and into the darkness they fell.

He threw his head back and roared, feeling the beast inside surface.

"Grab the blinders," shouted the male they called Azrael.

"Now," he commanded and again Elizabeth and Andrew joined hands. Oliver watched in awe as a golden haze erupted from their other palms, attracting the *Luz* dragon towards them. Azrael jumped on the beast and wrapped blinders around its eyes, causing it to sway and buck to dislodge him.

Ibis's breathing hitched, and arms held onto him. Squeezing as tightly as she could. As if this was her last moment.

His arms tightened in return.

"You protected me," she stated, in a whisper.

Nothing mattered. He didn't care if he had no past. The only thing that mattered was the present.

Was his little Ibis.

Was his future with her.

Was his mate.

"Always, my little Ibis. Never doubt that."

Chapter Fifteen
Purring Males

O liver rotated his shoulders, happy to be out of the new clothes provided to him by Azrael. He preferred his chest armor over the confounding button vest called a shirt. The leggings or pants fit comfortably and had convenient compartments on the side to secure items.

This he approved.

Selma gifted him with a cloak. Not just any cloak. An enchanted cloak to hide his wings when worn. She manipulated the fabric and wove in a spell similar to Azrael, which hid his skeletal form when worn. Ibis attached it to his armor. The heavy black fabric with emerald vines intertwined around a letter "V" for The Veil laid across his back.

"Can you change into gargoyle form?" asked Selma.

He arched an eyebrow at her curiously.

"I want to make sure the cloak shifts with you," she said, crossing her hands and twirling a finger around.

He stepped away from Ibis before his wings exploded from underneath the cloak. His skin changed to stone gray as his shoulders broaden. Eyes blazed and with a shake of his head, his horns extended to the back of his head. Razor claws protruded from his fingers. He smirked at his little Ibis's wanton stare. He glided to the floor, folding his wings behind him. The cloak was now gone.

Selma pressed a hand to her throat and cleared it before winking at Ibis. "At least we know it works."

"And he didn't split his pants," Andrew chuckled.

A sweet blush tainted Ibis's cheeks.

A rumble began in his chest. The one his little Ibis referred to as purring.

Purring.

He now understood the significance of this word. It was like what Chaos did when she was content. Although Chaos seemed to do this purring with everyone.

He would not.

He only *purred* for his little Ibis.

She placed a hand on his armor, checking the attachments of the cloak as he changed back to his sunlight form. Her flush face and warm touch enticed him. With a mind of their own, his hand slid low around her back, pulling her closer till they were nose to nose.

"Do you find the clothing to your liking?" His voice broke in a husky rasp.

Ibis blushed deepen. She smiled knowingly and raised herself onto her tiptoes, brushing a chaste kiss to his nose. He pulled back.

She kissed him.

Granted, it was not a full fledge declaration of the heart kiss, but the chaste kiss was affectionate.

And she had done it in front of the others.

In front of her closest friends. Those she considered her family.

Without hesitation.

Without fear.

His little one bestowed him with sweet devotion.

His purring grew louder. Louder than ever.

She leaned a hand on his chest and smiled up at him, snagging her bottom lip between her teeth. He tightened his hold on her, bringing her closer to him. His fingers flexed against her lower back.

He heard the snickers of Andrew coming from somewhere behind him, followed by a sudden slap.

"Ouch. Jupiter's balls, Elizabeth. That hurt."

"Then don't poke fun."

"Exactly," Selma said.

"I'm not poking fun. Just never heard anyone purr besides a cat."

Elizabeth sighed, and he only assumed Selma made some distorted face or other. He didn't care. He didn't bother to look. His eyes were only on Ibis and her loving smile.

"You're just jealous," Elizabeth stated.

"Of what?"

Selma laughed, "Oh Andrew, Andrew, Andrew. Don't you know? Males who purr are hot."

Ibis blinked and stared into the darkness. Azrael had assured her she was safe. She felt anything but that. Tyzion stood near, weapon in hand, along with Andrew and Elizabeth, in case the *Luz* dragon attacked. After discovering what book it escaped from, they determined it was the only one that had emerged from the pages.

Thank Goddess.

It was bad enough there was a kaleidoscope of butterflies swarming the library, a merman lounging in a private bath quarter and a woken devilishly handsome gargoyle hiding out in her loft. Ibis didn't know what else to expect.

A dragon was not one of them.

Frick frack.

She glanced around, not that she could freaking see anything in the darkness, but she glanced anyway. A warm hand rested on her shoulder. She closed her eyes and relaxed, eased by Oliver's touch. His closeness encased her, shredding any uneasiness she felt.

He had come for her and for once, she felt wanted.

Felt needed.

Felt treasured.

Felt, dear Goddess, dare she admit it, felt loved?

Not just the type of love shared among family members or the love shared among close friends.

The type of love she only read about in the books Elizabeth gave her. The type of love she'd witnessed between Selma and Azrael. The type of love she craved to one day have as her own.

Even before Oliver was released from his curse, she felt an overpowering sense of protection enveloping her every time she sat in his stone lap. A sense of yearning to belong in his arms. An enchanting moment in time forever engraved in her mind.

Ibis glanced back, placing her hand over his. Her fingers rubbing against his. Oliver's eyes smoldered, then returned to stare into the darkness, focusing on Azrael as he provided information on the *Luz* dragon.

"It is imperative the dragon remains in the darkness. Any light will alert it."

Azrael glared at Oliver. He then glanced at Ibis. She gave him a reassuring smile. "Of all the beings you fall in love with, it had to be a gargoyle," he muttered before walking away.

Ibis froze.

Not because it was ice cold and her body temperature dropped.

Or because she feared for her life, like earlier.

Oh no.

She froze because her frick frack supposed to be friend couldn't keep his skeletal mouth shut and thoughts to himself.

Goddess, she could use that watering can right about now.

Azrael turned and smirked.

Ibis glared back at him. She didn't care if he could read her mind. It was a gift a reaper had and one Selma had gained after mating with a reaper. Something Ibis thought was a brilliant enhancement to have.

Except for now.

It was as annoying as Andrew's singing, which he continued to do even though Elizabeth threatened to feed him to some mythical sea creature in Ronan's book.

Had she fallen head over heels, uncontrollably in love with Oliver?

Yes. Yes, she had. There was no denying her feelings for him. If she was honest with herself, during the Bring Forth spell, it was him who crossed her mind the entire time she recited the spell, not whoever Mr. Book-Boyfriend was.

But now they needed to figure out how to complete the Return-Back spell and each time she thought of it, a small part of her heart broke off and crumbled, leaving an emptiness inside her. A loneliness she knew far too well before Oliver came to life and into her world. A life she wanted to share with him.

Ibis just didn't know how she could do it. Selma researched her tomes and came up with nothing. Azrael had not come up with anything either, except for a *Luz* dragon. Elizabeth and Andrew also could find nothing in their relics.

Oliver's presence weighed heavily on her mind.

"You are troubled, little one." Oliver's voice caressed her skin as he leaned in and whispered into her ear. "What has you so concerned?"

Ibis nibbled her bottom lip, tears stinging her eyes. She hated crying. She was not one of those who could pretty cry. Her cries were straight up, a snot running, red nose, whimpering mess. She blew an unladylike breath from her lips, trying to accomplish two things; dry up the tears threatening to leak from her eyeballs and lighten the mood. Neither seemed to work. She made it worse.

Strong hands gripped her hip, gently turning her to face him in the darkness. He tucked his head, keeping his eyes cast low, lest the glow of his eyes trigger the menacing dragon. "Do not fear the giant lizard. I will not let it harm you."

Ibis released a strange noise between a giggle and a whimper. She would not fall apart now. She leaned her head against his chest, breathing in his familiar scent. A scent that reminded her of the pine candles she had mixed with something stronger.

Spicier.

Earthier.

Masculine.

A mixture she found soothing and enticing.

As she shook her head and peeked up, something halted her. Oliver moved. His cape swished around her, morphing into his wings. They wrapped around her as his arms reached out and pulled her back into his body, lifting her off the ground and into the air. She gasped at the sudden feel of weightlessness. Her arms reached out and took hold of his arms. He held her in the air.

"What is it?" she asked, searching the ground and hating she could not see in the darkness. Her fingers itched to snap a flame. She hesitated, knowing it could alert the sleeping *Luz* dragon.

His arms held her close. Closer as he held them above in the air. "There is another," he uttered in disbelief.

Another?

"Another dragon? Where? We need to warn them," she struggled to turn in his embrace.

"Not another dragon," he muttered, sniffing the air.

"Ibis, are you alright?"

Was she? She didn't know? Oliver was acting strangely. It wasn't everyday she was swept off her feet into mid-air. With her free hand, she reached over and searched in the darkness for him. Connecting with his neck, she made her way up to his cheek, drawing his attention back to her. A slit of purple hues glowed down at her.

"Tell me what's wrong."

"Ibis?" Azrael called out again.

She groaned. "One second," she sing-songed, as if whatever was happening was normal.

With pleading eyes, she focused into his half-opened eyes.

Oliver closed them, resting his forehead on hers. His lips brushed hers tenderly. The sturdy ground appeared below her feet as he lowered them. "Even in eternal stone sleep, I will forever be yours, my little Ibis. Never forget that," he whispered in her ear before releasing her into Azrael's arms. Something silently communicated between Oliver and Azrael. She sensed it, right before Oliver flew out of her grasp.

Her heart stopped.

"Oliver!"

The sound of her voice crying out his name tore through Oliver as he flew out the heavy doors swiftly, avoiding any light to seep in and down the hallway. Elizabeth and Andrew were trailing behind along with Tyzion, but he couldn't wait.

"Goddess!" someone shouted from the hall. He ignored the cries and raced to the library.

Arriving at the doors, he hovered.

Adrenaline fueled him to charge through the doors.

Instinct warned him to tread carefully.

Oliver's hands opened and closed. With a deep snarl, he pulled his wings back and pushed them forward, rushing the door with a gust of wind. The heavy doors of the library flung open, releasing a painful screech. He lowered himself to the floor, unsheathing his claws, and tucked his wings behind him. Blue mist spread across the floor eerily, leaving a slick residue on the surface. Water roared from the arch, rushing up and around the stones and back down into the abyss over and over.

His ears twitched, listening to odd sounds. From behind, he sensed Elizabeth and Andrew, followed by Tyzion. Tyzion walked over and stood next to him.

"There's something here," he said.

Oliver nodded, eyes peering into the haze. He tilted his head and opened his hands. Cool mist teased the inside of his palms.

"Do you see anything?"

Oliver shook his head. "No, but he's in here."

"He?"

Oliver nodded again. This time he felt him.

He was close.

Too close.

"I will see if I can seek him out," Tyzion said, unlatching the cape he wore. He pulled back the hood from his head and what was once a man standing before him now was a mere shade. A phantom blending into the surroundings.

Elizabeth and Andrew walked forward, careful where they stepped. Their hands joined and eyes glowing. They glanced around the room, inspecting the area.

"Careful Tyzion," Elizabeth whispered, as Tyzion floated away.

"I can't sense the familiars," Andrew stated.

Oliver stopped.

Within the shadows, large wings flapped, causing a tunnel in the mist. Yellow eyes glared back at them. A long tail swished up from the floor, snapping close to them as a warning.

The gargoyle was taller than Oliver. He came out of the shadows holding Chaos, rubbing her belly contently.

Chapter Sixteen

Charlie

I bis glared at Azrael.

Not just glared.

Oh no. She radiated heat from her big brown eyes that if she could absorb the energy forces around her and shoot them out of her eyes, she'd aim it right at his bony head.

"That's not nice, sweetheart," he muttered.

Frick frack!

"Stop reading my mind."

"Stop threatening to shoot laser beams at me."

She sliced her eyes back and fisted her palms.

"You're going to pop a vessel if you keep that up," he teased her.

Ibis snapped. "How do you tolerate him?"

Selma smiled lovingly at Azrael. "He grows on you."

Azrael chuckled, walking behind Selma and placing a gentle kiss on her shoulders before reaching behind his head and pulling the cloak over, transforming his skeletal face to what he would look like in human form. His long hair hung over his shoulders and a smirk teased his lips.

"Will you go already and check on Oliver since you won't let me?" she shifted on her feet, ready to pace the dark room. Of course, not that it would work for her. She couldn't see a frick frack thing in there.

Ibis couldn't wait to come face to face with that stubborn, crabby, overprotective, handsome gargoyle of hers. She most definitely was going to give him an earful, not to mention the coldest shoulder ever. How dare he just leave her behind like this? She didn't care that it was because of the intruder in the library. She could have helped. She's a frick frack witch, for Goddess' sake.

"Ibis, it's safer for you to stay here and let him handle the other gargoyle," Selma said.

Gargoyle?

"Another gargoyle? Is that who's in the library?"

Selma looked at Azrael, who growled and bowed his head.

"You two need to stop your silent communication and spill it."

"We will discuss this later, mate," his red eyes glowed with a bit of humor and something darker that Ibis knew was a message not meant for her. From the looks of Selma's smile under the reddish hues, it was a discussion Selma was more than willing to have.

"Ibis," Azrael began, and she interrupted him.

"He knew, didn't he?"

A sigh of resignation escaped Azrael. "He's trying to protect you. We don't know if this N.O.T.W. is a friend or foe."

Jupiter's balls. If this gargoyle escaped from a book, who knows what else is making its rounds in her library?

"I need to get back there."

"No," Azrael stated.

"You don't understand," Ibis persisted.

"I understand, sweetheart, but I promised him I'd protect you with my life, which is the only reason I did not go down there myself and instead sent Tyzion."

Selma sighed and interjected. "You and I both know Ty can handle whatever situation arises. He's more than capable. You do not always have to be first to respond."

It was an aged old argument among the two. Azrael took his role as head of The Veil Force seriously, rarely giving up control. He relinquished some of that control after meeting Tyzion, who had since been his second in command.

"We will not rehash this discussion, mate."

Selma smirked, knowing she would win the disagreement. She stood before Ibis, blocking her non-existent laser beams.

"Selma, please," Ibis pleaded.

Selma's head titled, "You're worried about your familiars."

Not just them, Ibis thought to herself and winced, knowing Selma could read her mind.

Before Ibis could say anything else, the doors swung open. Ronan's golden scales shimmered down the side of his neck over his ribbed abs, slipping deep into his low riding sweats he borrowed from Andrew.

"Where is she?" he demanded. His voice was hoarse, filled with cool authority.

Ibis blinked once and then again. Selma raised her hand and placed it over her chest, toying with the heart locket with an appreciative grin.

"I can see why Elizabeth is infatuated with the Merman," she muttered to Ibis, ignoring Azrael's growl.

"Ronan, stay in the bath quarters," Ibis said. "It's not safe for you to be seen out and about."

"No," he frowned and sniffed the air. Something she learned Oliver did often. Did their world smell differently to them as well? "I worry about her safety. My princess must be kept safe."

Princess? If Elizabeth heard Ronan refer to her as a princess, she would float to the clouds in pivotal happiness.

"I'll take you to her," Azrael said, rolling his shoulders and no doubt his eyes as well. "You two will stay here," he pointed at Ibis and Selma.

"I make no promises," Selma chimed back.

"Neither do I," Ibis said, crossing her arms.

Azrael opened his mouth, then closed it. Then turned to Ronan, who only blinked his golden, unnatural eyes and shrugged his shoulders.

"I'd rather face the *Luz* dragon in broad daylight than deal with stubborn women," Azrael muttered.

"Careful mate," Selma singsonged, skipping behind him while holding the locket around her chest. "I can arrange for that to happen."

"Yes, dearest love of my life. I'm well aware of your capabilities." Faster than anyone could have expected, Azrael disappeared into a cloud of red smoke and reappeared before Selma. Arms formed out of the haze and wrapped around her, embracing her, before he reappeared in his skeletal form. The hood on his cape had fallen back from his head, revealing his true form. His voice was low and smooth, growing huskier with every word. "But there is no need to go to such lengths when you hold my heart in your hands," he whispered, laying his hand over hers and the locket.

Ibis looked away as if witnessing an intimate declaration of love that she should not have been a part of. Closing her eyes, Ibis inhaled a steady breath before peeking with one eye.

Azrael leaned forward as Selma's arms came around, pulling the hood over his head, transforming him. She ran a slim finger down his cheek before laying her hand on his chest over his heart. They shared a quiet conversation before he nodded.

"Stay close, love of my life. Do not stray far from me," he warned. Placing a quick longing kiss on Selma, he released her and grabbed his scythe, twirling it in the air. Selma reached over and grabbed Ibis's hand with excitement.

"Ever been through a portal?"

Ibis's eyes rounded, mouth dropped and part of her jumped with giddiness while the other part of her was frick frack freaking out. She watched amazed as Azrael continued to swirl the scythe in the air, causing a surge of energy to electrify the room wondering if any of this would wake the *Luz* Dragon.

"Don't worry. It's dark light. The dragon cannot see it," Selma reassured her. She bit her lip and tossed her lock of dark curls behind her shoulders. With a final twirl, Azrael raised the scythe high in the air and sliced downward, tearing a fission down of the energy source churning in the room.

Gentle hands pushed Ibis from behind, urging her and Ronan forward until they stood next to Azrael. With red eyes radiating heat, he secured his scythe over his shoulders and removed his hood, evaporating into red smoke before their eyes. He surrounded them with his red fog, encasing them. Selma spun around in circles, enjoying the chaos.

"Hold on to your wicked tits," Selma cackled, right before being zapped into the fission and out of The Veil Force room.

Oliver chased after the gargoyle, flying through the aisles, making the shelves rattle as books flew off and slammed on the floor. Sooty zoomed passed, screeching and flapping her wings with her perky white beak wide open as if smiling with glee.

Bookshelves toppled over, slamming into one another, creating a cascading domino effect. The items on the shelves slid forward, and either toppled to the floor or hung dangerously close to the edge.

"Sooty, no," Oliver chastised, catching the stubborn feathered beast and holding her close to his chest. "We do not eat butterflies."

Sooty let out a small bark and shriek, folding her wings in front of her, snapping her beak shut, disappointed.

Oliver flew back and placed her on her perch, and pointed a meaningful finger at her like a petulant child. The feathered miscreant rolled her eyes at him and settled on the perch, turning her head around to avoid eye contact.

With one last glance, Oliver shook his head and went back to the shelves, moving them back to their place and cursing as multiple items collapsed to the floor. He growled at Sooty and her mocking hoots, picking up the mess and placing them in a stack. No doubt his little Ibis would not be pleased with the mess they have created. Maybe he will blame it on the wretched, feathered familiar.

A smirk teased his lips. He huffed a deep breath and glanced up at the ceiling, watching in dismay as the visitor still hovered above, chasing the little winged friends. With a push off the ground, he flew straight up and blocked the raid. His wings expanded, shielding them from the assault. His eyes glowed and claws extended, pointing directly at the other gargoyle, who looked at him, confused.

"We Do Not Eat Butterflies," he said, annunciating each word with purpose.

The gargoyle stared back. His yellow eyes glowing brightly before blinking and acknowledging. They simultaneously glided down till they both touched the ground. Oliver felt the flutters of little wings behind his wings. He looked behind him and found several butter-flies hiding behind his wings. He reached over with his hand. One Monarch, with beautiful orange and black wings, perched itself on his fingers. Its delicate wings waved gently back and forth till it fluttered up and landed on Oliver's horn.

Elizabeth and Andrew made their way from one of the other aisles after picking up the mess left behind. She slammed several books down on the desk, followed by Andrew, who looked up and snickered at Oliver and the butterfly.

"Ah, you made a friend," he teased.

Oliver growled and rolled his eyes up to see the butterfly flutter its wings faster, as if delighted by the friendship. The other gargoyle took a step closer to Elizabeth. His eyes glowed brighter. Oliver moved to place himself in front of him.

"We do not eat them either," he warned.

The gargoyle whined and shoulders slumped forward. "I do not understand this place. Do they not eat in this world?"

Elizabeth squealed, "Don't eat me. Here," she said, shoving her brother forward, "you can eat him."

"Hey," Andrew complained, taking multiple steps back as the gargoyle's eyes widened and mouth opened, showing off hungry fangs.

"No," Oliver said sharply. "We do not eat them. They are family."

The room grew still.

Oliver glanced over and caught Andrew's goofy smile as he placed his hand over his heart and Elizabeth's soft eyes.

"Awe. Not only are you cute, but you're sweet too. Like a big squishy marshmallow," Elizabeth said with a sigh, pretending to squish his cheeks in mid air.

Andrew snorted, "Don't worry Oliver, you get used to her after a while."

Oliver tilted his head. "You didn't call me Charlie," he mumbled, almost afraid to ruin the moment.

For a human, Andrew had a firm grip. He placed his hand on Oliver's arm, squeezing tightly. "Course not. You're Oliver," he said reassuringly. Mischief danced in his dark eyes before he nodded towards the gargoyle with his head. "He's Charlie."

A loud roaring laughter erupted from Oliver. He couldn't remember the last time he lightheartedly laughed with such merriment. Maybe he never had.

"I do not understand the humor. What is this Charlie word?" the gargoyle asked, standing tall.

Oliver recovered and held a hand up to reassure him, but Andrew had other ideas.

"It's a name," he said casually. "His name is Oliver. My name is Andrew," he pointed to his sister, "This is Elizabeth. She's a pain in the ass, but you get used to her."

Charlie looked confused. His piercing eyes glanced at Elizabeth and then he quickly turned to stare at his ass, raising his tail and feeling for any pain. "She has caused me no pain in my ass."

Elizabeth covered her mouth from laughing.

"Jupiter's balls. It's a figure of speech, Charlie," Andrew grumbled under his breath.

Oliver crossed his arms over his broad chest. At least he was not the only one who did not understand completely the mundane world. He should interfere. Explain things to the garg...er... Charlie.

Charlie huffed. His wings trembled in agitation. "You make no sense, human. Elirabell caused me no pain in my ass,"

"Elizabeth," she said, correcting him in between his rant.

"Elirabeth," Charlie repeated.

She walked closer, pointing to her lips and pronouncing each syllable carefully. "E-liz-a-beth."

He repeated after her, mimicking her mouth's movements, "E-liz-a-beth," he drawled.

She smiled, turning to Oliver and Andrew. "Nice job Charlie."

He stood up straight. His eyes glowed. A small smile hinted at his lips.

"Don't worry," she whispered to Charlie. "Andrew is a pain in my—"

"Not that again," Andrew grumbled.

Charlie groaned.

At that moment, Oliver decided it would be best to take Charlie away from the menacing twins. They would drive anyone mad.

"Are you sure we cannot eat them?" Charlie asked.

Oliver glanced at the ceiling and groaned as Sooty terrorized the fucking butterflies again.

Jupiter's big frick frack balls.

Chapter Seventeen
Ugly Butterflies

A fraction of a second paused and Ibis passed through a portal of red haze. Familiar lights and sounds came forward as another fission opened and they crossed through the arch. The arch from the center of her library, which she stared at wondering where it would lead to. The same arch with a raging funnel swirling around from the abyss below and around to the other side, spinning around and around, creating blue smog to spread around the floor.

What in the world was going on? Lightning crackled from the edges of the Arch. Ronan's eyes rounded as he stared into the water. His hands reached out and captured the raging water. His golden scales glowed as if the water energized him with strength. Small slits on the side of his neck expanded while he took deep breaths. He glanced down at her in awe and turned to the waterfall.

Elizabeth's giggle broke his trance. There was a deep grumble following her. Ibis did not recognize it.

Ronan's hand swung out from the water, splashing drops all over the ground. The sounds of crystals scattering on the ground drew Ibis and Selma's attention. Ibis picked up a startling blue stone and then another. Selma found more, and they put them all together in a small satchel.

"He did something to the water," Ibis stated, staring at the stones, perplexed. Selma studied them, just as confused. A problem for another day.

Azrael pulled his hood over his head and waited. He pointed his finger to thin air. Tyzion appeared. His hood came over his head.

"Report," Azrael commanded.

"All is well. Charlie will harm no one," Tyzion stated.

"Charlie?" Ibis and Selma both asked.

Tyzion nodded his head. "The twins named him. Better yet, Andrew named him, right after Oliver declared to Charlie they could not be eaten since they were family."

Ibis melted.

Her heart swelled.

"Although they are driving Charlie mad with their constant bickering. I think Oliver might reconsider it."

Goddess!

Ibis handed the stones to Selma and pushed past a laughing Tyzion, who continued to report to Azrael. By the time she located them, her eyes rounded, then sliced at the disastrous mess of her books and lopsided shelves.

Oliver shuffled his enormous feet. The warm somersaults in her belly tumbled over and over, watching him stand still while butterflies perched on his head, shoulders, and wings. His eyes glowed at the sight of her.

"We can explain," both Elizabeth and Andrew exclaimed.

Ibis crossed her arms over her chest and tapped her foot. She wished she could set someone's hair on fire. Even just a little bit.

"If you set someone's hair on fire, let it be his," Elizabeth said, knowing her too well.

"Why me?"

Elizabeth rolled her eyes. "I have better hair than you."

Andrew sneered and bumped her with his shoulder, only for Elizabeth to come back harder and knock him over.

Ibis had enough and grabbed the first book from the counter and tossed it at them, which only just bounced open and released an eclipse of moths.

"Oh no!" Ibis cried out, racing to shut the book and stop the kettle of moths from escaping. "Sooty," she called out in a panic.

"*Hooot*," she replied, sweeping low and capturing one moth in her mouth.

Ibis smiled at her little friend. "Remember when I said no butterflies?"

Sooty opened her wings wide and bounced up and down.

"These you can eat. Go feast," she said, watching Sooty blink and soar around the room and up to the ceiling like it was an open buffet with no wait line. "You too, Kit."

Kit ran around the library, hopping on top of the bookshelves, enjoying the open hunt, while Chaos swatted any moth that flew close to the ground. Rosie did not seem to care. She remained quiet in her little bed, curled up, lifting her nose in the air.

Large wings cast a shadow on the surrounding floor. Ibis glanced up and gasped. It was the other gargoyle. He flew around with Sooty, enjoying the moths and the chase. Warm arms pulled her up and wrapped around her. Soft, fluttering wings tickled the side of her face as a butterfly landed on her hair. She raised her finger and let the Monarch perch itself. Beautiful colorful wings opened and closed before it flew back to her hair.

"Charlie?" she asked.

The rumbling of Oliver's laughter made her smile. "It is a good, mundane name."

Sooty screeched, and a roar from Charlie followed it. "I guess she has a new friend."

"Hmm," he mumbled, not looking at anything else but her. "He will help Sooty. Better he eat the bad butterflies than family."

"Moths," Ibis corrected. "They are not bad butterflies. They're just not good for libraries with old tomes, scrolls and books. They will eat the pages."

Oliver glanced up at the moths. She couldn't help but chuckle. "Go join the chase," she encouraged.

His eyes lit up, then his chest rumbled. "They can chase. I have what I want right here."

Book of moths secured...check.

Sooty laid out in a food comma...check.

Charlie seated on the ground and in awe as Chaos meowed and purred her way through a book explaining things to him...check.

Elizabeth and Ronan making out in some dark corner in her library...frick frack...check.

Andrew making gagging noises over said make-out session...check, check, check.

Ibis flipped through the next spell book and slammed it shut.

Nothing.

She blew the string of hair out of her face and tapped her finger on her desk. There had to be something. Ibis organized the books on her desk and shuffled them into her cart. A cart she swore was empty earlier. Why was there a book on myths and lore? She picked up the heavy book, flipping through the pages and stopped short. She stared at the page that hovered in the air. Ibis placed the book on the desk and examined the page from each side.

The page discussed guardians. Specifically gargoyle guardians. Ibis's heart raced and eyes consumed the words written. She read the captions. Flipping the page, she consumed the next section and then the next. Page after page, she read everything listed.

Everything documented.

Everything transcribed.

And yet, in each section, the image of the guardian was missing. The one detail that solidified her suspicion was the description of purple eyes.

Her Oliver was a guardian. He had mentioned it once before. But he just wasn't any guardian. He emerged from this book. This frick frack book sitting on her desk with the missing image of him.

A sadness washed over her.

It was a lore book.

Myth.

He did not have a past to go back to.

An existence.

He would just go back to being an illustration in a book tucked away on her bookshelf. Ibis's eyes stung with unwanted tears. It was unfair. She felt his presence before she saw him.

"My little Ibis," he gently said from behind her, reaching around and pulling her close to him. His wings encased her in his embrace. "Your sadness troubles me."

She sniffed and tried to wipe the tears away, turning in his arms. "I don't want to lose you."

He hummed, leaning his head against hers. "There is nothing more that I want in this lifetime than to stay and spend it with you. A thousand times over my little one. This," he said, reaching over behind her and picking up the book, "has no meaning to me." He let it fall with a loud thud on the table. His hands cupped her cheeks, bringing her tear stained face up to his. "I do not care what myth, lore, legend was written about me. I do not care that I do not have a past. I do not care that I was non-existent. I only care that I have a future with you, my little Ibis. You are my reason to exist in this world."

Ibis held him tight.

"You are my life. My world. Even if I did not come from those stories you love to read, enchantment brought you into my life. You're my magical ever after." His voice was rough with emotions.

Ibis wasn't sure if she laughed or cried. Maybe it was both. Her arms laced around his neck, holding tight as he lifted her off the ground. "It's happily ever after," she said.

His purring grew louder and arms tightened around her. "That too."

She snuggled closer, burying her face into his neck, breathing him in. A sense of tranquility filled her from head to toe. His fingers brushed through the long tresses of her auburn hair. Ibis closed her eyes, relishing the feel of being held closely. She kicked her feet up playfully, enjoying the weightless feeling.

Oliver slowly lowered her to the ground. Her feet touched the ground and a sudden thought came to her mind. "The page," she whispered.

Ibis snapped her eyes back at Oliver, and he tilted his head over at her. "What if we got rid of the pages that you belong in? If we remove the pages you belong in, you won't be sent back into the book.

She chewed her lower lip and glanced around, looking for Selma. "It could work Oliver. I just need to check with Selma."

Knots twisted and turned in Oliver's belly. Something told him it would not be that easy. Getting rid of the pages sounded like a reasonable resolution, but doubt plague his mind. It seemed too easy to be true.

The spell needed to be performed. They needed to return Charlie back. They needed to return Ronan back. They needed to return the Luz dragon back. Not to mention the insane amounts of bad butterflies that were still lingering around the ceiling and threatening to escape from the book within his little Ibis's desk.

It needed to be done. He swallowed the large lump forming in his throat. He stared at Ibis as she explained her idea to Selma with enthusiasm and excitement. Azrael glanced over at him. Oliver no doubt knew the Reaper was reading his thoughts. A solemn look crossed Azrael's face, which caused Selma to glance his way. They both knew this was a long shot.

Ibis hurried back to him, with Selma close behind. "Ibis is not wrong. It could work. The sooner we try to fix this, the better. We are getting close to Ostara and the last thing we want is to have the Countess involved," Selma said.

"Does Charlie need to go back?" asked Andrew.

The room remained quiet. In the short time Charlie was with them, they grew to enjoy his company. He was larger than Oliver, and yet he seemed more childlike. Sooty adored him. Chaos was in love with the gargoyle, and even though Kit and Rosie didn't seem to have formed an attachment, they were sad to see him go.

Oliver tensed.

He sniffed the air. His eyes grew large and eyes glowed.

"They must both leave," said a voice they were all dreading to hear.

He growled and hissed, turning his figure around and expanding his wings, shielding them. Family *Tia Isa* was back, and she was not alone. That wretched weakling, Elton, and two other females accompanied her. The one female had her arms crossed and wore a smug smile. One he was not sure he liked. Her sleek, long, dark hair shined under the library's lights against her fair skin and dark eyes. She stared at him. Unphased. The second female stood further back, a bit and unsure. Her luscious ebony hair flipped and curled in different ways and teased her shoulders.

"*Tia Isa*," Ibis said with a slight tremble.

"Do not speak," Countess Isa sneered, pointing her long thin finger with a manicured nail at her. "You thought you could keep this from me? All of you? I know everything that happens at The Veil. Everything," she said, loud and furious.

Oliver glared at her, standing close to his little Ibis. It aggravated him to the core, watching the smug smiles cross Elton's face and the long hair female.

"Elton, bring me the book. I will put an end to this," the Countess said, not bothering to address Ibis.

"Wait," Ibis pleaded.

Elton took two steps forward and stopped. He raised his hand and with a flick of his wrist; the book snapped shut and flew to him. Appearing bored, he walked backwards, looking at Ibis up and down. It infuriated Oliver even more.

"Can I eat this human?" Charlie asked, standing next to Oliver.

"You may," Oliver replied without hesitating.

A delightful chuckle rumbled through Charlie.

"Countess Isa, if I may," Selma began, stepping before Ibis, moving her back. A voice trickled into Oliver's mind, sounding like Azrael, warning him to keep Ibis close. The Countess glared at Selma but remained quiet. "With all due respect, the spell was called upon by the Power of One. It will need to be envoked the same way."

The Countess folded her arms and snubbed her nose in the air. "Are you challenging my decision?"

Oliver listened, edging closer to Ibis. His ears tweaked at the small noises around them. Noises he became too familiar with. Like the sounds of Sooty taking flight and picking up the watering can. The sounds of Elizabeth and Andrew joining hands and the energy sizzling in their palms. Or even more, the sounds of Tyzion, lowering his hood and phasing into his phantom form to hide among the shadows.

"I am not challenging you at all," Selma said.

"She's right *Tia Isa*. You cannot complete the spell."

"I brought him here," the Countess hissed. "I will send him back."

Oliver snapped his curled tail on the floor. "You brought me here, but not on your own. You do not have the power to send me back."

Countess Isa's face remained blank for a second. Just a second before a menacing look crossed her eyes.

"You may be right, gargoyle but, I can curse you back to stone-sleep."

"No!" Ibis shouted right before an ice-cold sharp pain struck his chest.

Chapter Eighteen
Enchanted Madness

C haos.

       Not Chaos, her adorable familiar, who Ibis adored.

No. It was utter chaos in the library. Beginning with that toad's wart, Elton, who thought he was some Cosmic God, because of the flicking wrist magic he did to get the lore book. Followed by Selma going toe to toe with Tia Isa, which, if Ibis was honest with herself, was pretty frick frack glorious.

And that was only the beginning of the chaos. Again, not her little familiar, Chaos. Although she played a role in the chaotic mess.

It happened so fast and yet slow at the same time. This is how Ibis knew Elizabeth and Andrew were using their magic. They manipulated time.

She blinked, feeling a drafty breeze from her eyelashes. Her gaze gradually sought Oliver, who reached for her instantly as if unphased by the slowness in time, securing her safely behind him. A leisurely smile teased her lips as she stared at him, then her eyes grew round as Sooty appeared from the aisles carrying the blasted watering can. Beak wide open as if smiling.

A fraction of a second later, time sped up and resumed. Sooty smacked Elton's head, causing his eyes to roll backwards, and he collapsed on the ground. Mona squealed, reaching for Regla's hand. Instead, she found nothing by air. Regla crossed her arms and ignored Mona, shaking her head and rolling her eyes. "I will not be a part of this. I told you that before. Your hatred and jealousy is ridiculous. I will not standby and watch you hurt them."

It was then Ibis saw it.

Tia Isa's contorted face. The way she glared and fumed. She slammed the book Elton brought her down, causing a ripple to explode from the contact, throwing everyone near to fall back. Tyzion brought his hood over his head and caught Regla as she flew backwards. Mona landed next to Elton. Oliver and Charlie raised their wings up and blocked the blast from those behind them from getting hit, but it wasn't enough to shield the bookshelves, desk and chairs. One by one, bookshelves trampled over with books sliding down. Each one trembled as if something wanted to come loose.

"No," Ibis whispered, aware that everything was coming alive in the books.

Her desk rumbled, and the drawer flew open, releasing a large eclipse of moths followed by a kaleidoscopic of butterflies. A tornado or colorful wings swirled around the center of the library.

The water around the arch raged, releasing a river mixture of mist and frigid water, seeping into the floors. Ronan's scales illuminated before he scrunched low to the ground and released a vicious bellow. A sound Ibis had never heard.

"Something is coming up from the waters," he warned them. Ronan grabbed Elizabeth and raised her out of the water, placing her on the upturned table.

Ibis refused to take her eyes off of *Tia Isa*, whose hands were swirling in front of her. Her mouth moved silently, as if reciting a spell.

"No!" Ibis cried out right before *Tia Isa* released her hands and shot Oliver with her magic. A roar erupted from his lips, tossing his head back. His wings expanded as he came out of the water and into the air. Pain etched in his rigid form.

"Oliver," Ibis called out, climbing the spiral stairwell. She called out his name, ignoring the lightning flashes and the sudden cries of her friends below as large tentacles came out of the mist.

Oliver finally collapsed onto the railing, causing them to shake. Ibis helped him over and brought him into her loft. She laid him down, running her hands over his chest where a spiderweb of veins spread slowly over his body.

"Stay with me," she pleaded. "Don't go. Stay."

His hand came up and brushed her warm tears. His once beautiful glowing purple eyes faded. "Do not cry, my little Ibis."

"Ibis!" Selma cried out for her from below.

She closed her eyes, letting the tears flow. Letting all the emotions release from her soul.

"Little one," Oliver's voice faded. "You must complete the spell."

She shook her head. "No. I can't. I won't lose you. I can't lose you, dammit."

"Ibis!" Elizabeth cried out, fear imminent in her voice.

"Oliver, you can't go. You can't go back into darkness."

"My little Ibis. I'd spend an eternity in darkness knowing you are by my side, then living and never have known you."

Her head dropped against his. His body stiffened. Heavy as he laid there on the ground in her loft.

"Hurry little one. Our family needs you," his voice fading.

"Ibis!" Andrew called out, panicking.

She let out a cry, reaching for Oliver's face. His lips smiled sadly at her, blinking heavily. Her lips touched his, fusing tightly. Feeling the warmth fade.

"*Hooot*," Sooty quietly said, flapping above them, dropping a small bottle with a mixture in it. Ibis stared at it and then at Sooty's solemn eyes. She perched herself on Oliver's shoulder, leaning her feathery head against his, and closed her eyes. Kit crawled over, shivering and tucked herself under Oliver's arm, snuggling closer into him while Rosie and Chaos both laid across his chest.

Ibis leaned over once more, staring into his fading eyes. The solidifying web of veins crawled up his neck and, little by little, made their way over his chin into his cheekbone. They had spread all over his torso and into his arms and onto his wings.

Her lips brushed his. It was the softest of kisses and yet it said everything that needed to be said and still she couldn't let him go without him hearing it. "I love you," she whispered against his stone lips.

She watched his eyes round at her admission right before they faded.

Leaning back, she took the bottle Sooty brought her and placed the mixture in her hand. Energy surged in her palm .

"Oh my Goddess, it's a *luz* dragon," someone shouted from the hallway.

Thunder clapped within the library, and a loud roar consumed the hallway.

Ibis snapped her finger, producing one small flame.

"By this light,
I ask the Goddess for her might,
To reverse thy magic recited,
And return back their souls guided.
A singular spell bro..ken,
By the Power of One who spoken."

A soft breeze blew the flame out.

The tornado of butterflies and moths disappeared.

The Luz dragon vanished.

The mist and raging waters of the Arch went back to its normal tranquil flow.

Ronan was gone.

Charlie was gone.

Oliver was gone. Deep in stone-sleep. That was till Ibis went to touch his face and he began to fade.

Her eyes rounded.

"NO!" Desperate anger flowed through her blood.

"Ibis you did..."

Ibis's red puffy eyes stopped Selma from finishing her sentence. "He's go...ne."

Selma rushed over and embraced her. Holding her tight in her arms, leaning her head into Ibis's. "I know, sweetheart. I know."

"No. I mean, he's gone, gone. He's fa..l..l..ing apart," she said.

Ibis saw it when it hit Selma. Her green eyes filled with tears. She released Ibis and ran over to the ledge. "Andrew," she called down, "is Oliver in his page as well?"

Ibis waited, but she knew in her heart something was not right. She looked at Sooty, who bounced up and down. Selma snapped her neck around at Sooty and then back around the ledge. "Elizabeth, Andrew, come quick," she said before running back to Ibis and kneeling next to Sooty. "Are you sure, Sooty?"

Sooty kept bouncing up and down.

Ibis looked at Selma, confused.

"The Power of Four," Selma said quietly.

Ibis blinked. The Power of Four? Frick frack. She could not be a part of The Power of Four. She barely could do the Power of One.

Selma placed a hand on her shoulder. "You can do it. You won't be alone," she said, turning and finding a soaking wet Andrew and a broken-hearted Elizabeth.

"I'm so sorry, Elizabeth," she whispered.

Elizabeth shook her head and rushed over to her, embracing her tightly. "It had to be done."

Andrew wrapped his arms around the two of them and looked down at Oliver. He sniffed and closed his eyes.

Sooty, Rosie, Kit and Chaos all took sides next to Oliver and lowered their heads.

"What is going on?" Andrew asked.

"Oliver did not return to his book. He's fading," Selma said, rubbing her fingers together as gray stone crumbled from Oliver's body. Ibis whimpered while Elizabeth gasped. "We can fix this with The Power of Four."

Andrew sat back on his knees. "Fuck Jupiter's balls."

Ibis wiped the snot from her nose and grimaced.

"I'm in," Elizabeth said without hesitating.

"Elizabeth?" Ibis whispered softly.

"Hey, if one of us deserves a happily ever after, it should be you."

"You deserve one too."

Elizabeth smiled sadly and squeezed Ibis tightly.

Selma crawled around Ibis and yanked Andrew down. The three of them kneeled behind Ibis and lowered their heads. "When you're ready, place your hand on him."

Ibis didn't think twice. She reached over and placed her hand over his wound on his chest, where the wicked stone webs began and bowed her head. Selma placed her hand on Ibis's shoulder and a wave of power moved through her body. Ibis took in a sharp breath as she felt Selma's energy flow through her. Suddenly, Andrew laid his hand on her other shoulder and Ibis felt the flow rush on her other arm. Selma let out a little gasp, feeling the same surge. Elizabeth placed her hand on top of Selma.

Suddenly a ray of light exuded from their hands, partially circling them. Ibis closed her eyes, willing the circle to close. "It's not working," Ibis sadly cried out. "My magic is not strong enough."

"Then try with me," Regla said, coming up the stairwell. "It would still be the Power of Four. You will be our anchor."

"Regla, if you do this, you will sever your match with Mona," warned Tyzion.

"Good. It's the best thing that could ever happen to me."

Ibis gave her a soft smile and nodded. Elizabeth shuffled over as Regla quickly kneeled next to Ibis. Reglas' eyes immediately transformed to golden embers. She placed her hand over theirs and instantly a charge of electrifying force surged around them, closing the circle.

"Be happy Ibis," Elizabeth whispered.

Ibis smiled and closed her eyes, willing whatever little magic she had into their joined hands. A brilliant purple glow erupted around them, seeping through Oliver's stone figure.

Call to him, Ibis heard Selma whisper in her mind.

Please Goddess, let this work.

"Oliver, come back to me."

She loved him.

This was worse than darkness. What's worse than darkness? The feeling of non-existing. Which is actually worse than never existing at all because in this case it's the knowing of non-existing that sucks Jupiter's balls.

Funny, Oliver never got around to asking why everyone wants to suck Jupiter's balls.

That was beside the point. His little Ibis loved him. He heard her right before the fucking darkness took him under. Her sweet declaration. He took it back. Knowing he non-existed was not the worse part. It was knowing he could not rage, roar, fight. Nothing. He was lifeless and yet still living.

His little Ibis.

Even in sorrow, he couldn't just be.

If he thought about it, he could pretend he could feel her. Sense her. Maybe hear her. But that was not the case. He was alone. Only felt the thawing of coldness ease from his muscles. See a sliver of light in the distance.

That can't be.

Were they the witches again? Did family *Tia Isa* do something to his little Ibis?

Damn curses.

Damn witches.

But that wasn't what he was hearing. His ears twitched. Wait. His ears twitched. As in, his ears actually twitched. He felt the sensation of them twitching. Muffled voices came through the sliver of light.

His eyes focused on the light. He could see it. He stared at it, worried it would fade away and leave him in the darkness again. Oliver tried to move his limbs, but they were still numb. He tried to say something, but he was still silent.

A warm hand brushed against his chest.

Goddess, that touch. If he wasn't terrified of losing the light, he'd close his eyes and savour her touch.

His little Ibis was near.

A sudden pulse rushed through her palm into his chest, right to his heart. It zapped his organ like a lightning bolt. Another one followed a second later, and then a third one. His inside began to heat, bringing life back into his soul.

Then he heard a whisper of a call, so soft, so melodic, it drew him to it. Like those sailors, he read about to a Siren's call.

"Oliver, come back to me."

His little Ibis. She was here.

Ibis held her breath. Gone was the crumbled statue. Laying before them was her Oliver. Living and breathing. His eyes were closed, his skin slightly pale. She brushed her knuckles down his cheek. Her little familiars sat patiently waiting, all holding their breaths.

"Did it work?" Andrew asked.

Selma watched intently, as did Elizabeth and Regla.

Come on, come on, come on, Ibis kept chanting in her head.

His curly tail flinched, swishing around and slapping on the ground hard. He winced and furrowed his brows together. His eyelids moved and steadily they opened, showing her the most vibrant, glowing purple eyes she loved.

Chapter Nineteen
Ostara Ball

I bis looked at the picture drawn of Charlie and smiled. Holding it up, she found the perfect place to hang the photo of him. Oliver grabbed it and flew to the upper wall and attached it to the nail. She still found it funny, Oliver flying around with a tool belt. He seemed to enjoy having the mundane tools and also insisted they have multiple watering cans placed around the library for security.

Who was she to argue with him?

Besides, this evening was the Ostara Ball and Ibis was excited. Not only was it her first ball, but she would attend with Oliver. They have been the talk among The Veil. The new "It" couple. Many asked where Oliver came from. Selma and Azrael came up with a story for him and even gave him a last name, Libro, which meant book.

After the enchanted madness, as Oliver referred to it, Ibis and her friends..er..family cleaned up the library. Of course, a little magic was used. Not that she performed any of it. She was done with doing magic. Ibis had happily come to terms with being a librarian slash familiar keeper slash master gardener. She truly didn't mind. Sure, she could do minor spells but the big stuff, the stuff that could release *Luz* dragons from books and tornado butterflies, she was out.

No, thank you.

Not interested.

Well, maybe a little interested, but no. No, thank you.

"Little one," Oliver called out, flying down to their loft. He had changed into an outfit Selma made from her magical spindle. It made sense why Azrael could turn into his red smog and come back and still have his clothes intact. What better person to design Oliver's clothes, then Selma herself? Selma practically jumped for joy when Ibis asked if she could design a suit for Oliver.

The suit fit him perfectly. The dark charcoal gray tailored pants tapered around his form, leaving room for his tail to be free. It remained curled, which annoyed him, but since Ibis found it adorable, he seemed inclined to leave it alone. He still hated wearing a button-up shirt. Instead, Selma designed a vest, covering his torso with an area on each shoulder for his cape to attach.

"I'm almost ready," she said, grabbing her earrings and placed them into her lobes. She felt his eyes on her. She turned and blushed. His stare was intense. He had looked at her many times, but this look was new.

It wasn't everyday Ibis dressed up in a full length ball gown. Her hair was picked up with strands of long waves falling down her back from her ponytail. Her dress, a soft lavender ball gown, cinched her waist perfectly. Her bodice cut low enough to show modest cleavage and was completely beaded with amethyst stones and held up with matching straps on each side. The tulle skirt was full and rimmed at the bottom with ruffles.

She flattened the front of her dress and looked down at everything and back at Oliver. "Do you like it?"

He remained silent and walked over to her. More like stalked over to her. She took small breaths till he stood in front of her. He really was devilishly handsome in his gray vest and tapered slacks.

She reached over and fiddled with the button on his vest and made sure his collar was all the way down. Nervously, she glanced up, "You clean up nice."

He tilted his head and brought up his hands, which held two gardenias. "I read it was costumery to give a flower when going to a dance."

She snagged her bottom lip between her teeth and nodded, fighting back the sting in her eye. She took one gardenia and placed it in the pocket of his vest. The other one, she placed in her ponytail, securing it with the one-hundredish bobby pins she wore.

Oliver tucked a finger under her chin and raised it up to meet his eyes. She happily raised her gaze to his and smiled.

"I love you too," he said, softly placing a kiss on her lips.

She whimpered and held onto him while he deepened the kiss, only to end it quickly. "We must go, or you will not make it to the ball."

For once, she didn't give a frick frack if she went to the ball. Who cares?

He chuckled, placing a soft kiss on her nose. "My little Ibis, you are breathtaking." He twirled her around before drawing her back into his arms. "Alright my love, let us go to this Ostara Ball."

She pulled back and smiled sweetly at him. Ibis grabbed her invitation. As usual, his wings expanded from beyond the cape and he carried them both over the rail, gliding down till they reached the bottom level. He slowly let her slide down his body, capturing her lips again, before taking her hand and walking out of the library.

"By any chance, this wouldn't be one of those things where we will have to suck Ostara's balls?"

Oh, how she loved her gargoyle.

To say the Ostara Ball was magical was an understatement. Ibis couldn't have imagined the beauty. Selma outdid herself. The spring bouquets were everywhere. There was an entire wall, from floor to ceiling, encased with different seasonal flowers, ranging in pastel colors. Candlelights floated on the ceilings with roses wrapped around the candlesticks. Music ranging from the Old World to the New World played all night. Magical beings from both The Veil and Briar Solarium gathered together, enjoying themselves.

Ibis and Oliver had just left the dance floor when the doors abruptly opened and soldiers of The Veil Force charged in disrupting the dance. Azrael raised an eyebrow from underneath his cloak and walked over, standing in front of the guest.

"What is this?" he demanded. Tyzion came to stand on the left.

"They ordered us to secure the gargoyle."

There was a gasp and multiple whispering among the guests.

"The Ostara Ball has begun. We do not interrupt a solstice celebration."

"That is not your call," the one soldier said from the front.

Azrael leaned in, growling as he spoke. "Really? Then who's call is it?"

The soldier swallowed a nervous knot in his throat and looked away from the beaming red eyes.

"Mine."

Ibis looked at the doors. From the shadows, *Tia Isa* walked in wearing a stunning red gown, beaded head to toe with sparkling rubies.

"You have forgotten the code of The Veil Force, Azrael. He is a N.O.T.W. and needs to be apprehended."

Selma gasped and whispered, "That bitch," and stood next to her mate.

"I have forgotten nothing, Countess Isa. Oliver Libro has shown no threat to our world. In fact, Oliver has provided much information. Detailed information. Information that you will need to answer for."

Everyone mumbled as if struck. Ibis leaned into Oliver and squeezed his hand, then released it before facing her Tia. "*Tia Isa*, don't do this. Don't..."

"*¡Cállate!*," *Tia Isa* barked.

Oliver hissed. His tailed snapped on the ground as a warning. Ibis turned and laid a hand on his chest, calming him. He placed his hand over hers and looked straight at her Tia.

"That is not how you speak to family," he said. "That is not how you treat family."

"*Por favor*, what do you know about family?"

"More than you," Ibis said, disappointed.

"Yeah," Elizabeth said, coming from to stand beside her.

"That's right," Andrew agreed, joining them.

Selma smiled knowingly, as did Azrael. She turned to Ibis and winked. Ibis had no clue why Selma would wink at a time like this, but before she could analyze it, Seraphina flew in from behind her, *Tia Isa* causing an uproar. The glorious peahen landed right in front of Azrael and Selma.

"I've had enough. Seize the gargoyle for interrogation immediately," *Tia Isa* commanded. The soldiers stared at Azrael and Tyzion, torn.

Seraphina shook her feathers and lowered her head, bowing respectfully.

"Do not move," said a sweet voice from beyond the hall. Out of the shadows, a small, petite woman walked forward. She wore a simple forest green a-line dress. No beading. No glitz. No glam. Just classic. Her frosty white hair was in a bun above her head. A thin gold necklace hung around her neck with a small amulet.

Azrael reached behind his cloak and unsheathed his scythe. Twirling it in the air, he slammed it on the ground and announced, "We honor our High Priestess," to which everyone bowed their heads and repeated the same.

Tia Isa looked horrified. She glanced around the room and took two steps back.

"Do not move," the High Priestess said. She pointed at the guard, calling him over and whispering to him. He nodded and stood in front of *Tia Isa*.

"Countess Isadona Gil, we charge you with syphoning. Veil Force, take the Countess to the High Priestess chambers for processing."

Everyone in the room felt and heard the shock.

The High Priestess rose her frail arm in the air, commanding the room for the attention. "Ostara Ball is a celebration of new beginnings. It is the celebration of rebirth, spring and some may even say, a new start," she said while looking at Oliver and Ibis. "Let us continue the celebration," she said with a clap of her hands and a bright smile.

The music resumed.

Ibis nervously waited for the High Priestess. Once she was face to face with her, tears filled her eyes.

"*Pero cariño, ¿porque las lagrimas?*"

Ibis wiped her tears away. "I'm sorry abuela. I'm just...it's been..."

"*Si.* I know. *Bueno,* I know now. Your *Tia Isa* lost her way. Maybe it's time she found a new path. A new beginning."

Ibis glanced at the empty doorway. "She wasn't always this way."

Her abuela nodded. "Greed is an evil force. It can contaminate the heart and spirit of a witch," she said with a heavy sigh. "I warned her many years ago, *pero tu Tia-* "she paused, snapping her mouth shut and shaking her head, "when she broke her match with her sister, she did not realize the damage it did to her own magic. She would not listen. Isadona is well aware of the laws. Syphoning magic is forbidden." Solemn eyes glanced at Ibis. "As was Mona's behavior."

Ibis gasped. "But..."

"No. Mona is family. She should know better and will learn her lesson harshly. Maybe some time with the trolls will teach her a lesson."

"*¡Abuela!*"

"*¿Qué?*"

Oliver chuckled.

"Don't you think that's *too* harsh?"

"She's getting off easy. The trolls are a lovely community. *Bueno,* some of them are," she smiled wickedly.

Ibis chewed on her lower lip.

"Don't worry. *Ese saca moco*, Elton, is getting his as well. He's being reassigned to the crypt's stable."

Oliver tilted his head. Ibis giggled and explained, "The crypt's stable is where the reapers keep their skeletal horses. The smell is not pleasant."

Oliver's eyes rounded. "Worse than Jupiter's balls?'

"Very much," her *abuela* replied with humor in her eyes.

"Then who is going to run The Veil?" Ibis asked curiously.

Her *abuela* looked around, placing her hands behind her back and rocking on her feet. "I thought maybe we try something new. Something more modern. Something hip. Like the Power of Four with an Anchor."

Ibis's eyes bulged. "I can't do that. I mean, you don't want me to do that. I practically destroyed the library, released a dragon, created a magical disaster with flying insects and something came out of the mist and that was just from one from the spell."

Her *abuela* nodded, agreeing with everything. "Yes," she said proudly, "and you rectified it all as well. Plus, it was your touch that saved him cariño. The magic passed through you. It was your voice that called him out of the darkness."

Ibis turned and caught Oliver's sweet eyes on her. The rumbling in his chest grew. His tail swept out and curled around her waist.

"Well, are you going to finally introduce me or not?""

Ibis laughed, heat flushed her face. She turned and intertwined her arm in Oliver's. "Oliver, this is my *abuela*, Manuela, High Priestess of The Veil."

Oliver looked at Ibis. "She is family?"

Ibis smiled. "She is family," she confirmed.

"She is good family?"

Ibis chuckled.

"I am the best family," her *abuela* said with a sassy smile. "Come closer. Let me look at you."

Oliver leaned over. Her *abuela* placed both hands on his cheek and stared into his eyes. She turned his head to the side and then the other, before releasing him and giving him a great big smile. "He is a good one," she said proudly.

Ibis looked up at Oliver, gleaming with joy. "Yes. Yes, he is."

Her feet were screaming at her. They ached and throbbed. She kicked off the tortuous heels and let them fall where they lay. Glancing around, Sooty sat perched in her little bird cage, snoring away, while Kit and Chaos both were curled in the same bed, snuggling with Rosie. She made a mental note to buy another similar bed or bigger one for the three of them.

The sounds of wings flapping caught her attention. She looked up and smiled. Oliver glided down to her in full gargoyle form. He landed in their loft and reached for her hand. She wasn't sure what he was about, but she took it anyway. The smile on his lips should have been a warning.

Within seconds, he lifted her off the ground and sprung her into the air, cradling her close before he flew them out the balcony doors, into the night.

"Where are we going?" she asked, enjoying the cool breeze on her skin and the smell of fresh pine air mixed with spring flowers.

"Hold on tight," he whispered, flying higher into the sky.

Don't look down, don't look down.

She trembled, and he squeezed her closer till he stopped ascending.

From where they were, she could see The Veil and the town. The old haunted manor and the creek that ran behind it.

"What are we doing all the way up here, big guy?"

"Your family *abuela* is right. The Power of Four may have given you the energy source, but it was you who saved me. You who brought me out of the darkness. There is no reason you should doubt yourself."

"Maybe," she whispered.

"No. No, maybe."

"You're being feisty."

"Feisty? This word I know, but that is not what I intend to be. I intend to be honest. I intend to be loyal. I intend to love you no matter what your decision is."

"Oliver," she whispered.

"I brought you up here, to the stars, so you can see for yourself. The way I see you, my little Ibis. That among them, you shine the brightest."

"I love you," she couldn't resist. She kissed him, holding him close.

His arms tightened as he returned the kiss deeply. Both exchanging unsaid words and emotions with just their action.

"Promise me one thing?"

He nodded, nuzzling her neck.

"If I ever get doubtful again, you'll bring me here."

He leaned forward and kiss her lips sweetly, "Always, my little Ibis. Never doubt that."

Author's Note

A special thank you to Britton Brinkley, Bobbie Isabel and Ashley Willow. Thank you for being on this witchy-monster ride with me. Your words of encouragement, laughs and friendship mean the world to me.

To the rock-star Isabelle Olmo, thank you, thank you, thank you for the amazing cover. You brought Ibis to life. She is very special to me.

To my sister, thank you for always reading everything I toss your way, even when my ideas are a crazy train wreck.

To my husband. My rock. My love. Thank you for believing in me and for being my happily ever after.

About the Author

Award-winning author Gracie Cooper was born and raised in South Florida to a family so big and boisterous you'd think they were hosting their own carnival. Gracie's childhood was all about the weekly domino games and Sunday feasts that brought everyone together. Nowadays, Gracie calls the outskirts of Saint Augustine home, where she lives with her husband, two mischievous sons, and a miniature schnauzer who think he's the boss of the household. But just because she's a little more settled down doesn't mean she's lost her love for a good party – in fact, she'll never turn down a chance to play a rousing game of dominoes or gather her loves ones around the table for a delicious meal.